# Lock Down Publications and Ca$h Presents

# TIL DEATH 3
# Who Will Bleed

## Aryanna

First Edition October 2023

Printed in the United States of America



Lock Down Publications
P.O. Box 944
Stockbridge, GA 30281
www.lockdownpublications.com

Like our page on Facebook: Lock Down Publications
www.facebook.com/lockdownpublications.ldp

# Stay Connected with Us!

# CHAPTER 1

*Leroy*
*March 2028*

"Bly, step to the front, you made bail."

While the cop's announcement had been expected, it still didn't carry with it the appropriate joy for someone being freed. Incarceration was nothing new to an old vet like me, but this brief trip behind bars had been completely unexpected. Normally I got the handcuffs put on me for some serious shit that carried mandatory minimum sentencing guidelines, but that wasn't the case today. My arrest this time stemmed from a motorcycle I'd borrowed being reported stolen, which seemed innocent enough, but it wasn't. I was too rich to steal a fucking bike, and too smart to get caught with it if I DID do it! The bike in question belonged to my lawyer's husband, and she'd given me permission to use it. He hadn't though. She got the black eye, and I got the cops called, which made her husband a whole bitch in my book. There was no time for me to be mad though, because all of this was a smoke screen and distraction meant to divert my attention from the acts of war being levelled against me. Two of the people I trusted most in this world had betrayed me, and the fact that I never saw it coming is what made that blade cut the deepest. IG trying to negate my contributions, and take the power I'd amassed within the Nation of Rulers motorcycle club that I'd help found, was a betrayal that shouldn't have surprised me. Powerful men always wanted more power, and absolute power corrupted absolutely.

The betrayal from my wife though... I was still struggling with processing the shock I was feeling from all that I'd learned about what my wife Gini had been doing behind my back. The love and loyalty I'd given her was the kind that changed lives, and I thought it had changed ours for the better, but I was wrong. I was so fucking wrong.

"Collect your personal affects at the front desk, and here's your next court date," the cop said, handing me a slip of paper.

I followed his instructions, looking over my shoulder the entire time because I knew the feds were waiting to fuck a nigga's day up. After signing the inventory sheet for my phone and my money, I was escorted to the main lobby, where I was surprised to find my lawyer waiting.

"Where are the feds?" I asked, stopping in front of her and scanning the lobby.

"I already took care of that and I let them know you wouldn't be voluntarily sitting down with them to answer any questions about the half a kilo of fentanyl they found in your food truck. You don't operate that truck personally, so you don't know how it got there. As for the gun, well, it doesn't have your DNA or fingerprints on it, so there ain't nothing to talk about there either. I kindly convinced them of how bad it would look on the evening news for me to do an interview about the blatant harassment and government corruption directed at you. From that point, they agreed not to approach you or apprehend you without concrete evidence of wrongdoing on your part," Erin replied.

Erin Gilse was a bulldog of a lawyer, and more beautiful than your favorite rapper's main chick. Her best attribute was her loyalty to me though, and right now, I needed that more than anything.

"Well played, Counselor. Now let's get the fuck out of here."

I pulled her to her feet and followed her outside into the bright afternoon sunlight. My head stayed on a swivel, looking for threats, because this moment was the best time for my opps to try their hand at knocking me off the board.

"Where's your car?" I asked, looking for a familiar vehicle to go to.

"I got a rental through my firm because I was too paranoid to drive my car, or anything belonging to you. It's right here though," she said, holding up the key fob to shut the alarm off.

The pearl white 2028 BMW IX looked sleek and expensive, but not so much as to bring the attention of a car jacker.

"I'll drive," I offered, taking the keys and helping her into the passenger seat.

I got in and started the engine, but I just sat there for a moment and tried to slow down the chaotic thoughts playing 5-on-5 basketball in my mind. It had been a long time since I'd been in a place of such complete disarray that I couldn't organize the moves I needed to make on the fly. I considered myself a King of adjusting to shit in real time, but I wasn't feeling like that at the moment. Despite my outward calm, I was panicking inside.

"Are you okay?" I asked, looking over at her.

"No. I'm fucked up, L, and I'm scared."

"I get it, but you're not alone in this because I'm here with you. I'm scared too, but I'm here," I said.

"You're scared? Wow, I don't think I've ever heard you say that."

"Yeah, well, you never told me that you were carrying my child either," I replied, chuckling.

"So that's what's scaring you in all of this? Me being pregnant? So do you. I mean, if having the baby isn't something you want, then—"

"Don't even think about saying it, because it's not an option. No, we didn't plan this, and I had no idea it was even a possibility, but we're here now. That baby, OUR BABY, deserves a chance to be born, and we need to make sure our child has the best life possible. Can you commit to that?" I asked, reaching for her hand and squeezing it gently.

"I'm in this with you, but realistically, you need to know that this shit is going to be HARD, and it's gonna get harder."

I knew that what she was saying was even more so true because of her husband, but I couldn't worry about him right now.

"We'll get through ALL of this, I promise," I vowed.

She squeezed my hand back and gave me a small smile that at least conveyed some faith. I couldn't ask for more at this particular moment. I pulled out of the parking lot with the intention of going somewhere safe to strategize and create a plan to work with.

"Is your house still occupied?" I asked.

"Yeah, he's there, but the kids are with his mother. I know my eye looks bad, but it's okay, and he won't hit me again, so—"

"You know that's a lie because this ain't the first time he's hit you. I'm not thinking about that though. I was just trying to find a place for us to set up shop, regroup, and figure out what to do next," I explained.

"My house is DEFINITELY not the spot."

"No, it's not. I can't trust any of the known Nation of Rulers safehouses until I know who's gonna side with me against IG," I said.

"Do you think he KNOWS that you know he's coming after you?"

"That all depends on whether Gini knows that I know she betrayed me, because she'll probably turn to him for help. It's her best bet if she wants to stay alive," I replied bitterly.

"You need to make some calls and temperature check the situation. We can do that from a penthouse owned by my law firm in downtown Richmond," she offered, leaning forward to input the location into the car's GPS system.

Within moments, I had directions to follow, but as soon as I hit the turn signal to make a left at the light, the back windshield exploded into pieces.

"Get down!" I screamed, immediately jerking the steering wheel to the right and merging back into traffic.

Car horns sounded off in angry protest, but that didn't drown out the boom of rapid-fire gunshots echoing. I sideswiped a minivan, pushing it into another lane, but that didn't make me take my foot off the gas pedal I had mashed to the floorboard. I could hear bullets knocking chunks of fiberglass off of the fast-moving BMW I was pushing. I still couldn't see the shooters though.

"Stay down, Erin!" I ordered, weaving through traffic while checking my rearview mirror.

A black Cadillac Escalade was on my ass, chasing us, and there was a vicious-looking assault rifle in the hands of the nigga leaning out of the passenger side window.

"L, take this!" Erin said, thrusting a pistol at me.

"I can't shoot and drive, bitch, so just hold on and stay down," I replied, fishtailing around a corner.

I eased off the gas to allow the tires to catch traction, and when they did, I floored it again. I spotted an exit that led to a highway entrance and I made that my target, hoping to just outrun the truck. I hopped two lanes and tapped the brakes so that I didn't roll us into the guardrail, but I could tell that I was still going too fast. My split-second decision to avoid the on ramp made me change lanes again, and that's when I felt something hit me in the back hard enough to cause me to lose control of the steering wheel. I managed to not wreck, grab the wheel, and keep driving, but now the pain had my vision wavy.

"Oh my God, Leroy! Baby, you're BLEEDING!" Erin yelled, scrambling back up onto the seat beside me.

"Stay down," I said, coughing and fighting against a pain that was unspeakable.

I could taste blood in my throat, and I knew my lungs were in danger of filling up with blood from the gunshot wound. Still, I fought through the agony and drove like my life depended on it. I could still hear gunshots, and it took me a minute to realize that they were coming from Erin. When I glanced at her, I saw tears and determination on her face as she let her gun kick and scream like a newborn out the back window. I spotted a cop car at the intersection we were running down on, and I made the only decision that made sense.

"Hold on to something," I instructed as I hit the brakes and yanked the wheel sideways.

The car went into a perfect drift maneuver before smacking into the side of the cop car. For a second, I heard sirens, and Erin yelling...then I heard nothing and everything went black.

Aryanna

# CHAPTER 2

*Leroy*
*3 days later*

Even with my eyes closed, I could feel people in my presence, but I didn't feel like I was in danger. My ears and nose immediately placed the sounds and smells around me, alerting me to the fact that I was in the hospital. The excruciating pain radiating throughout my body told me that death HAD to have been close, so under the circumstances, I couldn't be mad to be laid up healing. Like most street niggas, I hated hospitals until I needed one to save my muthafuckin' life. With my eyes still closed, I took stock of my body's injuries based on the amount of pain I felt. The fragments of my memory provided the info that I'd been shot at least once in the back, and I'd wrecked the car I was in intentionally into a cop car. I tried to mentally access the events after that, but there was nothing more than a huge void, and that sent trickles of fear down my spine. A sudden image of Erin in the passenger seat beside me, dumping bullets out the window at whoever shot me, forced my eyes to open in this moment. I searched frantically for her to be somewhere in the room with me, but I was in a private hospital room by myself. The door was open and I could see people passing by, stuck in their own world, but my eyes locked in on the two men in suits posted up on either side of my doorway. They didn't look like feds, but they were strapped, which meant more than likely they were security for me. That meant somebody in this cruel world gave a fuck about my safety.

I needed someone to protect Erin and our unborn child though. I got ready to open my mouth to ask where Erin was at, but the taste of stale blood on my tongue told me that I hadn't used my voice in a while. I wouldn't be loud enough to get anyone's attention. I was able to move my right hand to hit the nurse's call button, and I did that without wasting time. Within a few moments a thick, beautiful, caramel-complexioned woman with brownish-red hair entered my room and pulled up to my bedside.

"Welcome back, handsome, how are you feeling?" she asked, smiling down at me as she checked my vitals on the monitor beeping.

"Hurts," I croaked out, painfully clearing my throat.

"That's understandable because you were shot, AND you were in a car accident, but they're giving you the best dope in the house, which should help a little," she said, winking at me.

"Where is my-my family?" I asked in a gravelly tone.

"Your family? I don't know. Have they been notified that you're here? I'm just your daytime nurse, but I haven't been introduced to your family in the past three days," she replied.

"Three d-days?" I asked, surprised that I'd been unconscious that long.

"Yeah, it's been three days since they brought you in, and the only people I've seen are the two dudes posted like sentinels outside your room. Do you want me to ask them about your family?" she offered.

I gave her a subtle nod, which prompted her to retreat to the door and exchange words with the men. When they looked past her to find my eyes open, one of them moved in my direction, while the other pulled a phone from his suit jacket pocket.

"Your emergency contact is being notified, sir, but we've been instructed not to let allow you visitors at this time," he said.

"Who ARE you, and who told you this?" I asked, slightly annoyed at the audacity of this lil nigga.

"My name is Benji, and my partner by the door is Malikye. Our employer was the one who gave us those instructions, and any questions about that, you'll have to direct to them. We were put in place to keep you safe from anything, or anyone, that appears to be a threat. Our orders are, shoot to kill," he replied in a matter-of-fact tone.

"Shoot to KILL? Hold up, I'm here to save lives, not become a victim in my own damn emergency room," the nurse said, putting her hands up, looking slightly distressed.

"What your name, Nurse?" I asked, bringing her attention back to me.

"My name is Latisha."

"Okay, Latisha, I want you to listen to me. Nobody is gonna hurt you, okay? Just keep doing your job, and I'll make sure you're well compensated," I assured her.

She looked from me to Benji, and then back to me, before nodding her head and retreating from the room.

"Who's your boss?" I asked, projecting as much strength into my voice as possible.

"I work for Mrs. Gilse and another unknown party, and that's all I'm really allowed to say because that's all I know."

"Where's Mrs. Gilse? Is she okay?" I asked, trying to sound mildly concerned while fighting the rising panic in my chest.

"My partner is attempting to contact her now to make her aware of your awakening, sir."

The amount of information that this nigga didn't know, or wouldn't speak on, was starting to piss me the fuck off, and I gave no fucks that this wasn't a rational response on my part. I wanted answers right the fuck now!

"Has my family been here to see me while I was unconscious?" I asked.

"To my knowledge, sir, Mrs. Gilse has kept all communication with anyone outside of this building regulated to video communication only."

"Yo, Benji, she's on her way," Malikye said, sticking his head in the doorway.

"What's her ETA, Kye?" Benji asked.

"Unknown at this time, but it was suggested that we lock down this particular floor now since he's awake, and be ready for evacuation," Malikye replied.

"Did you call in the necessary manpower?" Benji asked.

"Yeah, we've got two six-man teams en route, and everyone is licensed to move heavy machinery," Malikye replied.

"Excellent, but make sure they don't show up brandishing their guns. We don't wanna scare the white people...like last time," Benji said, shaking his head at the memory of something past.

"I got it, I got it," Malikye said, stepping back out into the hallway.

I had even more questions on the tip of my tongue ready to be asked, but I had to swallow them because someone looking like a doctor chose that moment to make his grand entrance.

"Good afternoon, Mr. Hawkins, I'm Dr. Demetri Edellson. How are you feeling today?"

I looked from the tall, broad-shouldered, bronze-complexioned man in the lab coat who'd been speaking to Benji and back, trying to figure out who hell he was calling Mr. Hawkins. The fact that the confusion I was feeling wasn't radiating from Benji gave me a feeling of unease on top of everything else.

"I'm, uh, I'm good, Doc. Well-rested," I replied hesitantly.

"I bet. From the looks of your charts and your vitals, you're healing extremely well and at an extraordinary rate. The two bullets that hit you in the back damaged your left lung and kidney, but we were able to perform emergency surgery to go in, remove the bullets, and sew you up before you could drown in your own blood. Your broken leg came as a result of the car crash, but I can say without the shadow of doubt that you'll dance again soon," Dr. Edellson said, smiling confidently.

"Well thanks, Doc. When can I get out of here?" I asked impatiently.

"That depends on how long it takes you to return to normal lung function. Right now, we need you to remain here where you can access extra oxygen and medical assistance immediately when needed," Dr. Edellson replied.

"No disrespect, Doc, but I'd rather pay the money it'll cost to turn my home into a hospital than to stay here, so I'd appreciate you pushing my discharge paperwork through."

"Tell you what, Mr. Hawkins, let's do a quick physical examination first, and run you through the full body scanner to see what's beneath the surface. Then we'll talk again. Sound fair?"

"Okay," I agreed, lying smoothly just to get him the fuck out of my face.

I was leaving this muthafuckin' hospital REGARDLESS. He went to the sink in the corner of the room and washed his hands before returning to my bedside.

"Now, you're gonna feel some discomfort, and I want you to let me know if it becomes unbearable," Dr. Edellson said, using the remote attached to my bed to slowly change my angle until I was sitting up halfway.

Benji backed up until he was part of the wallpaper in the corner, but he was clearly vigilant of the what the doctor was doing, and that eased my anxiety a little. The physical exam consisted of him checking my wounds back to front to make sure I hadn't opened them and that there was no infection. He moved slow, but by the time it was over fifteen minutes later, I was out of breath and sweating lightly.

"You're doing good, Mr. Hawkins, and your wounds look to be healing nicely. I still want you to take it easy though, and try not to do to much moving for the next week. Your leg won't need to be evaluated for another 4-6 weeks, but it was a clean break so it should heal without issue."

"When can I start physical therapy?" I asked.

"Sooner rather than later, don't worry. I'll make you a goal schedule for your day-to-day recovery, which you'll get after your full body scanner exam. Someone will come get you to escort you to X-ray soon," Dr. Edellson replied, using the remote to return the bed back to where I was laying flat.

Once he left the room, Benji stepped forward out of the corner and came to my bedside.

"Sir, I can tell you that Mrs. Gilse has every intention of moving you from this location today. It was already expressed to us that should you wake up, you would be moved as soon as she gave the go ahead. Your final destination wasn't discussed at that time, but we'll keep you safe regardless," he assured me.

"You're former military, aren't you?" I asked.

His smile said so much more than words, and now I had another piece of the puzzle slide into place. It was clear to me now that Erin had went into the "emergency contact" escape plan I'd put together years ago. This meant that all bridges were burned in her mind, and we could only trust those who we'd killed for to obtain their loyalty.

"Thanks Benji," I said, feeling untold gratitude swell inside me for Erin.

Despite it being obvious that she was okay and on top of shit, I still wanted to lay eyes on her so that I could see firsthand how her and our baby were doing. Knowing that she and I were on the same wavelength in terms of me being out of sight and heavily guarded had me thinking about spots where we could go into hiding. I didn't know who'd shot me yet, but I was hoping Erin had learned something in that department in the last 72 hours, because that would influence the decision on our destination. I didn't wanna go into a manic psychological state where my mind was constantly cycling through the possible enemy threats to us. My enemy list had grown beyond my anticipation with the recent turn of events before I'd been arrested. I couldn't afford to drive myself crazy or slip up, so I had to take my time, and I knew that would be hard because all I had was time to think.

"Benji, what hospital am I in?"

"Richmond MCV, sir."

I processed this information quickly, factoring in just how big the hospital was and its location in the heart of downtown Richmond. I was hiding in plain sight, given the fact that I had nothing but enemies in the city of Richmond, but I had no doubt that Erin knew that. Undoubtedly, this explained the fake name, and why my security team had instructions to shoot to kill.

"Benji, I need you to do me a favor. Get my clothes and let's get me ready for a quick exit."

There was hesitation clear in his eyes, and I understood his indecision was because Erin had given him specific instructions. I was gonna have to make it make sense for the young gunner.

"Listen, when Mrs. Gilse gets here, she's gonna want to get me out of here faster than a NASCAR pit crew can refuel. I obviously can't just throw on some clothes and meet you all out front, so we need to stay ready, and then we don't gotta get ready. Feel me?" I asked, feeling slightly winded at having to speak so much.

It was clear to me now what Dr. Edellson meant about my lung function needing to improve. Talking that much made me feel like I was swimming with my mouth open, which forced me to speak slower so that I could breathe more. I'd never felt so weak or so vulnerable.

"I get your point, sir. Just let me have a word with Kye," he replied, heading for the door.

They exchanged words, with Malikye doing more nodding than anything. Benji finished speaking, then went to a chair in the corner of the room under the outside window and grabbed a black duffel bag. While he picked something out for me to wear, I worked on putting the bed back in a sitting position. The pain was serious, causing me to grit my teeth as it radiated from back to front like a fast-moving roller coaster in my body.

"Are you, uh, okay with me helping you get dressed?" Benji asked.

"I'm a grown-ass man who is confident and arrogant as a muthafucka, so shit like that don't gotta be asked. If I could do it myself, then I would, but since I can’t, let's get it done."

He seemed to visibly relax the more I spoke to him, but I wondered what Erin had told him to make him so uptight with me in the first place.

It took us about five minutes to get me into some gray sweats and a matching gray hoodie. I was wore the fuck out physically by time I laid back against the semi-soft hospital pillow. When I glanced at the door to my hospital room, I did so intending to tell Malikye to get me some water, but instead, I spotted Erin's beautiful face. The joy I felt was instant, and it exploded in my chest like the bullets that had ripped through my back. But it was short-lived when my brain finally registered why she looked so different, yet the same to me. It was the wheelchair she was confined to.

# CHAPTER 3

*Leroy*

My words failed me when I opened my mouth, so I closed my lips swiftly and cleared my throat.

"Benji, I need some water," I said, locking eyes with him in hopes that he'd get the message.

"Yes sir, I'll get it," Benji replied.

"I got it from here, Malikye," Erin said, using her hands to push herself all the way into the room.

Malikye took the same cue as his partner, which left me and Erin alone. Even though I didn't have the words, I knew better than to ask the typical dumb-ass question about how she was doing.

"I'm so sorry, Erin," I said softly, shaking my head almost like I was trying to deny what I was seeing.

"What are you sorry for, L? For making the quick move that saved our lives? Don't be. If you hadn't hit that cop car, then we would've been gunned down like animals in the street, so don't apologize to me, because you saved us. You saved our baby too."

Hearing this made me close my eyes against the tears that sprang up, but that didn't stop them from spilling over onto my cheeks. The fear of her losing the baby had been in the back of my mind, growing bigger anytime I fed it with the slightest bit of time spent dwelling on the possibility. I felt something loosen in my chest now that I knew my baby had managed to survive the first hurdle life had thrown their way. There would surely be more hurdles, but for now, I would savor this win.

"Th-The baby is good?" I asked, just to hear it again.

"Yes, and the heartbeat is so strong that I'm almost POSITIVE it's gonna be a boy."

"Oh lord," I said, laughing and smiling at the thought of finally having a junior to carry my name.

The sobering sight of her still sitting in that fucking wheelchair tempered my excitement though, and took the desire to talk more about our son or daughter.

"Okay, you gave me the good news...now give me the rest. Is it your spine?" I asked softly.

"It's not as bad as it looks. The doctors say that it's temporary paralysis from the waist down due to severe swelling around the third and fourth vertebrae. They spent two days running tests, but I made it difficult because I was more worried about the test hurting the baby than them helping me. You can save your breath if you're planning to lecture me about that. The bottom line is that there's no evidence of nerve damage or permanent paralysis. I can feel point pricks in both legs already, and I can move my big toes, but I was still told that the recovery time would take time and patience. Plus some light physical therapy."

"How much does your husband know?" I asked.

I knew and understood that I needed to prepare myself for the possibility that this tragedy could bring them closer, especially because he didn't know that the baby wasn't his. From what I knew about him, he always showed guilt and contrition after he hit her. So her being in a life-threatening situation so soon after he got physical with her would only magnify the "honeymoon" phase of their abuse cycle. It was sick, but my loyalty to her had allowed him to continued breathing, despite my instincts to bring about the contrary.

"Daniel doesn't know anything because...I left him," she replied.

"Wh-what?" I asked, sure that I'd misheard her.

"It was gonna have to happen at some point, L. I mean, there was no way I could pass off a little mixed baby as his. He's white, and he ain't dumb! So it was best to do it now before he knew I was pregnant, and while he was still feeling guilty for hitting me."

"What about your kids? They need their dad, and you told me that he was a great father, despite his shortcomings as a husband," I replied.

"He is a good dad, but one thing I NEVER want is for my boys to grow up thinking that it's okay to put their fucking hands on a woman for ANY reason! You're a great dad too, Leroy, and I know you'll teach my sons to become great men. Overall, it was the right move to make, and at least now Daniel won't be a target in this can of worms I inadvertently stepped into with you. I need him to remain safe - at least for my sons' sake."

The way she made her last statement, accompanied with direct eye contact aimed at me, let me know that he was still off limits for me to kill too. I COULD promise her his safety, but we'd always know that it was a lie, and this would've been the moment I had uttered it.

"Where are your kids?" I asked, shifting the focus.

"They're with Daniel, but we're gonna work out a schedule that fits our lifestyle demands soon. We did sit down with the boys yesterday as a family and explain that we're getting divorced. I needed to make sure they knew that it wasn't their fault, and that we loved them as much as we always had. Nothing could or would change that, so that was our message. It was hard on them, and that almost made me said fuck it and stay."

"Why didn't you? I would've understood and been as supportive as possible until that lie was impossible to tell," I said sincerely.

"Because that would've been the same thing as putting a Band-Aid on a .50 caliber bullet hole. I knew the moment that you and I started mentally seducing each other that my days with my husband were limited, and I was okay with that because I fell in love with you. I'm not okay with him dying because of the life I've chosen to attach myself to. That's not fair to him, or to our kids."

What she said was very rational and it made sense, but my focus went elsewhere.

"So...you're in love with me?" I asked, smiling widely.

"Fuck you, and focus on the issue at hand," she replied, laughing softly.

"You're right, but we ARE coming back to this topic of conversation. First things first: who shot me?" I asked, feeling the deliciousness of necessary revenge wetting my tastebuds.

"I'm almost positive that it was IG, but he didn't use the people that are loyal to him inside of the Nation of Rulers. He tried to keep his hands clean and the mask hiding his true intentions intact, but because we know what to look for, it's impossible. When I was shooting back, I was aiming at the black Cadillac Escalade chasing us, and I even managed to send the passenger shooting at us straight to hell. His body was recovered, and it was discovered that he wasn't in any criminal database in the U.S. He was originally born in Mexico, so there wasn't a whole lot I could dig up on him and his activities out here. The driver and the other shooters got away, and the only reason I know there were other shooters is because I saw their glowing gun barrels sticking out the window. While I was laid up in the hospital, I had time to reach out to a few friends of mine, and I got my hands on the traffic footage from when the shooting started. I watched from the moment the people in the Escalade engaged, to the moment we slid into the cop car and they pulled off. The thing that caught my eye were the two custom Camaros I spotted trailing the high-speed gunfight. They didn't get involved, but it was obvious based on their driving that they were there for the action."

"The Camaro Cartel," I stated, putting the pieces of the puzzle together.

"That's what I was thinking, and that's what made me reach out for SERIOUS help."

"That was definitely a smart move or your part. But how much does your brother know?" I asked.

Her response didn't come by way of words, but the look she gave me said enough. I'd met Erin's brother Matt years before my path ever crossed hers, and under much different circumstances. Deadly circumstances. Matt found himself in some serious trouble involving drugs that didn't belong to him, which found him in the same county jail as me, fighting for his life. Matt was a good kid from a good family, but he'd made the bad decision to earn some extra money by trafficking pills for some friends he went to college with. What started out as a few pills between friends turned into duffle bag varieties full of Oxy, Percs, ecstasy, and fentanyl that were being supplied by beautiful Mexicana women with fair enough skin to pass for white women. Before he knew what happened, Matt had sold his soul to the cartel, which came with a lifetime guarantee of loyalty reinforced with a Teflon bullet to the brain. He was beyond scared, but shit got all the way real for him when he got caught with 100,000 pills during a routine traffic stop. Matt didn't call his parents or his lawyer first. He called the number for someone connected to his connect and begged for a way out. That's when it really hit home for him that his "friend"" were anything but that.

Erin was in high school so she wasn't yet the brilliant legal mind that she would become, but that situation definitely influenced her. I knew enough about the law to be able to talk him down from his desire to commit suicide in the jail, and I had enough juice in the streets to make sure the cartel didn't question his loyalty. I spent hours with him strategizing his defense until he could spit the Fourth Amendment search and seizure procedure rights in his sleep. When I touched the streets a couple months later, I made sure to keep his name good, and I put a little fear behind it. I had a sit down with the friend of the connect that he'd called from the beginning, who turned out to be another scared little white boy playing gangsta. His girlfriend's family were the ones with the juice with the Sinaloa cartel. I played him close to get to his girl, and then I made her see Matt's value if the situation was played right. Once I had her interest, and her riding my dick like it was her new religion, I removed her boyfriend from the equation by killing him in the name of Matt. That made Matt's connections seem both lethal and lucrative. When I'd found out that the prosecutor was trying to push for the maximum sentence, instead of accepting the illegal search and seizure defense his lawyer and I had offered, I took care of him too. Everybody thought I was crazy, but I was clairvoyant, because I knew that the favors I was incurring with Matt and the cartel would add up later in life. When it was all said and done, Matt walked on the drug charges, and then he took the valuable advice given to him by going into the military. It made sense in my mind to push him this way because if shit ever went bad with the cartel, Matt had a literal army behind him.

Fast forward all these years later, add Matt's above-average intellect mixed with his determination and drive, and he'd made it to a two-star Brigade General. He'd seen war and death up close, and those things changed him as well, but on my end, it had made him appreciate the things I'd done for him more. So when I'd needed a good lawyer, he'd recommended his sister, who was the best. And when I'd come to him with a wild-ass scheme of how to break my wife out of prison, he'd told me exactly where and how to steal a tank, heavy artillery, and a predator drone. He'd been as loyal to me as I was to him, but the stakes were higher now because his baby sister was more than involved. I had no doubt that he'd help us, but the question was, would he try to kill me afterwards?

"How pissed is he?" I asked.

"I don't know that 'pissed' is the right word. I mean, you're family to him, so when it comes to going to war, you know he'll always back your play. As for getting his baby sister pregnant, well, let's just say you're lucky that you're already healing from bullet wounds right now," she replied, snickering.

"Wow, that mad, huh?"

"Be honest, Leroy, how many times did Matt tell you that you weren't allowed to put your dick in me? Even if I started it?" she asked knowingly.

"Whatever. I'll deal with that when we have time. What else have you learned?" I asked, sitting up slightly.

"I know the identities of those two Camaro Cartel members, and I put people on their trail to find their operations location in Virginia. Matt has his people keeping tabs on IG and Zuk, and both seem to be moving like everything is normal right now. IG even reached out to me because he hadn't heard from you directly. I was able to keep the attack on us off any news feed, social media sites, or official paperwork with the help of the feds because it's obvious that you're being targeted for death. As soon as I accused the feds of being complicit with these acts, they went above and beyond to show that this isn't their doing. The name Lorenzo Hawkins is yours temporarily, but it can be yours permanently...if you decide to go into witness protection."

"Wait, what? Why the fuck would they think I'd go into wit-sec?" I asked, bewildered.

"Because it's so obvious that SOMEONE wants you to quit fucking breathing, and they think there has to be a very good reason for that. If you die, then they don't get their man for blowing up that prison, which means there's still public outcry. They're willing to give you a new life, but you'd have to tell them EVERYTHING about your old life, because—"

"Ain't gonna happen. So what's next?" I asked, dismissing the whole idea.

"Well, IG and Zuk may be acting normal, but Gini is acting weird as fuck. Like, she's fishing for information, and that's weird because she could just call you directly. Candice got away from her the same night that she picked her up, and your mom hid her somewhere that I didn't wanna know about. Lia is hiding out with some girl named Kali, and I damn near had to have her shot to keep her away from this damn hospital. She said that Kali has them both off the radar, and she said you would explain later why all of this was happening. The only reason that I know any of this now is because I took all your personal stuff, including your phone, when you were admitted into the hospital and Lia happened to call. Do you wanna update me? Because it sounds like I'm missing A LOT."

"We'll get to that, I promise. Do you have a location on Gini and Dana?" I asked, hopeful.

Something flashed in her eyes, despite her efforts at concealment, and it tickled my senses in a bad way.

"What is it?" I asked once she didn't respond right away.

"It's just... I don't know where Gini is, but we'll find her. As for Dana... Leroy, I know you cared about her, and I'm sorry to tell you this, but...Dana is dead. Shot twice in the face at point blank range."

It was on the tip of my tongue to ask who had shot Dana, but that would've been a dumb-ass question. The only person she would've let get that close to her was Gini.

"Sorry to interrupt, but I brought your water, sir," Benji said, approaching my bedside and holding a cup with a straw in it out towards me.

I took it in my hand, but I didn't put it to my lips right away because the sudden dryness in my throat wasn't from thirst. It was homicidal fury.

"Benji, are your extra people here?" I asked, looking at Erin.

"Yes sir, they just arrived."

"Good. Get us the fuck out of here, and shoot anyone who tries to stop you," I ordered.

# CHAPTER 4

*Leroy*

*3 weeks later*

One would think that it would be impossible for a nigga who has done a REAL prison bid to ever get cabin fever after sitting in luxury for a few weeks, but they were wrong. Not being able to go anywhere was getting on my muthafuckin' NERVES! We'd been hiding out in the hills of Kentucky in a log cabin Dana owned that had everything anyone on vacation would need, right down to a hot tub and a sauna. It was cool for the first week, and maybe that was because my mind had been on helping Dana's chapter of the Nation of Rulers grieve and reorganize their leadership. By day 14, I was over the whole idea of hiding out, and I was ready to make the ground shake beneath people's feet from the wave of violence I was bringing. Somehow, Erin had convinced me to just wait a little longer because my inactivity was fucking up the mental of my enemies. I'd kept IG and Zuk in the dark about everything, avoiding them and allowing IG to think that his plan was working for the moment because I'd taken a step back from all Nation of Rulers business in Virginia. As far as everyone knew, I'd been in a car accident and broke my leg. I wasn't speaking on anything else just yet because I didn't know who was in on the plan to gun me down. Taking the time to heal from my ambush was looking more and more like retirement to those whose only dream was seeing me out of the way.

The power of greed was my friend and ally because it made muthafuckas' masks slip and allowed me to see who they really were. It was a different story with Gini though. When we'd first talked on the phone after I left the hospital, I'd told her to meet me in Kentucky at the house Dana had us hiding out in at first when I'd gotten her out of prison. She agreed to the meet. She'd never shown her face though. Her excuse had been that she was chasing down all the leads she had on Dana's killer because she felt responsible for her death. She couldn't come out of the cold until she avenged her death. When I questioned her about what happened to Dana and why she felt responsible, she'd spun me some story about her being face down in Dana's pussy in the car while they were parked in the hotel parking lot. That distraction resulted in somebody sneaking up on the car and shooting Dana in the face, but they didn't shoot HER because they didn't see her. When I relayed the story to Erin, we both acknowledged the possibility of it being true, but it smelled like bullshit of the highest quality. I'd run everything down to Erin that Kali had revealed to me and Lia, and then I had to damn near strap her down to the bed to stop her from hopping in a truck and riding around with an AK-47 looking for Gini. I'd NEVER seen Erin that mad before, to the point where she was literally crying tears and hitting me to let her go so that she could bury a bitch. It took me a while to get her to calm the fuck down and remember that she was carrying our baby who'd been through enough trauma since its conception.

Eventually we'd ended up spooning on the king-sized bed with me holding her stomach from behind as we talked about the future. It was an experience I'd never had with the other mothers of my children, so I cherished it. Her homicidal rage at Gini was understandable because she knew just how much I'd sacrificed for that one particular woman. Even without me saying it, she knew how much it hurt me to be betrayed by Gini. I wasn't ready to deal with all those emotions yet, so I kept my focus on keeping us alive and outmaneuvering my opps.

"You want some breakfast?" she asked, stretching as she got up out of the bed with slow movements.

Her voice shifted my thoughts to the present. We'd been doing physical therapy together since we got here, and the progress in both of us was obvious. I appreciated her progress in all its naked glory as she slid from beneath the cotton sheets.

"You know what I want for breakfast."

"Nun-uh, you woke me up in the middle of the night eating that," she replied, laughing.

"So that would make it a midnight snack, duh. I didn't hear you complaining in the slightest."

"And I never would, babe. My only complaint is that you're not feeding me the way that I am you," she said, smiling devilishly.

I responded by pulling the covers back to expose my naked body and taking my dick firmly in my hand. Her smile widened as her eyes locked in on my hand moving slowly up and down my shaft. When she saw that I wasn't simply teasing her, she stopped in her tracks at the foot of the bed, and then she crawled back up to me in a slow, seductive way. I got hard instantly watching her predatory stalking approach.

"No hands," she said, playfully slapping my hand away as she moved over top of her target.

For a few seconds she admired how my dick stood up under her intense eye contact, and then she let her tongue slither out and lay flat against the base of my shaft. I could feel goosebumps pop up all over my flesh as pure excitement rushed through my veins. When my hand moved in her direction this time, I found my wrist clamped in her vise grip, and she didn't let go.

"There are penalties for not listening," she whispered before wrapping her juicy lips around the tip of my dick.

The softness of her lips and the way she took inch after inch of me on the carousel ride of her tongue until I hit the back of her throat made breathing impossible. When she pulled her head back up in the same slow manner, using her tongue to lick from the base of my shaft to the head of my dick along the way, I had to fight to keep my spine on the mattress. I released the breath I was holding when she fully freed me from her jaws. Then I heard myself whimper in submissive desire when she let the spit in her mouth build into a pool and then let it drizzle down over her bottom lip, splashing the head of my now-pulsating dick until it slowly cascaded down my shaft. Before my breathing returned or I blinked to regain clear vison, she chased her self-lubrication with a perfectly-executed swan dive, mouth first, devouring my dick like her favorite candy. Our eyes locked, and I saw the determination in her as she caught the fast rhythm required for someone eating a melting popsicle on a hot summer day. The back of her throat was like an incinerator, pushing heat throughout her mouth like the devil's spawn luring me into the black unknown. The sound of her slurping echoed off the walls, but it could barely be heard over the prayers flying freely from my mouth.

I communed with God while she did the devil's work, sucking my soul into her being like complete possession was her ultimate achievement. I fought her, resisting the strong will and pull of her mouth's magic, but it was a futile battle. The way her throat expanded and collapsed around my dick over and over again reminded me of how a snake eats. The moment I felt me slip past the limitations of the average gag reflex, I felt my cum erupt inside her mouth with the force of a fire hydrant exploding. As soon as she tasted my special serum, the greed in her was triggered like hearing a starter's pistol, and the suction coming from her mouth increased drastically. Her head game was that PRESSURE, and I folded within it like a drunk in a bar fighting his alcohol addiction by sipping his liquor slower. After she drained me dry, she got up off the bed and stood over me admiring her work as I lay there dazed by the explosions still happening behind my eyes.

"That was a well-balanced breakfast, babe. Thanks," she said, licking the residue from her lips as she walked out of the room.

I couldn't do anything with the small amount of brain cells she'd left me with to function, so I just laid there. Before I knew it, I was fast asleep, but the smell of bacon under my nose woke me straight up. When my eyes opened, Erin was sitting on the bed beside me, holding my plate in her lap.

" Poor baby. Come on and rest yourself. I'll feed you," she offered, lifting the plate and motioning for me to lay my head in her lap.

I moved to her lap and laid my head down so that I could look up at her and talk while she fed me.

"You took advantage of me," I said softly.

Her laughter followed the fork full of eggs she guided into my mouth. I chewed thoughtfully, knowing that I couldn't bask in the afterglow of this amazing wake-up call I'd just received for too long. There was work to do.

"How is your back feeling?" I asked.

"I'm fine, babe, you don't have to worry. I've had full function of my legs back for the last week, and I'm already up to walking a half a mile daily, according to my Fitbit. I should be asking how YOU'RE doing, since your hardheaded ass cut the cast off early and had to get another one."

"It wasn't early. That's why they put a soft cast on it this time," I replied defensively.

"Whatever, Leroy. You threatened to shoot the fucking doctor if he didn't give you a cast that allowed you more flexibility, DESPITE it being too soon for that. I heard you when I left the room to go to the bathroom," she said, glaring at me accusingly.

I was smart enough to know when to concede an argument, so I simply smiled sheepishly and opened my mouth to the piece of toast with strawberry jam that she was pushing my way.

"Anyway, what's your next move, L? I know that you've been paying attention to the reports coming in from the people we have as our eyes in the street. Shit seems to be barely functioning without your guidance and finesse, and I sense a panic coming, like when the stock market acts crazy. I know that your natural feeling is to protect me and mine, but babe, you can do that without forfeiting the empire your blood, sweat, and tears built. That would crush you inside," she said, stroking my dreadlocks while she spoke softly.

Everything that she'd said was facts because in a nutshell, she'd checked my fear about the consequences of going to war. I was a warrior at heart, which meant making it shake whenever my hand was forced, but I wanted to do nothing more that keep Erin and our kids safe. Having her and the kids made retirement more enticing in a way that had never been imagined before. I'd known that marrying Gini came with love and excitement, but I also knew that I never would've been forced to pull one foot out of the streets and the games they played. With Erin, I felt like I had to go 100% legit - or as legit as I could. Essentially, that would mean my time as a leader in the Nation of Rulers was finished, and I didn't know if I was there yet with that decision. Doing nothing though would allow another nigga to make the decision for me, and then I'd be at his mercy. The streets weren't merciful.

"You're right, babe, but I do see a solution where I can have it all," I confessed.

"Tell me what that means, L. To have it all means what?"

"Honestly, now it means being surrounded by the people I love, being financially secure, and being safe. Realistically, I'll never stop looking over my shoulder because I can't. Once you've taken a life, you have to forever expect that bitch karma to come restore balance within the universe. No one is bigger than that, and we're not untouchable. For that reason, I think it's always important to keep an army at my fingertips, but I know you don't wanna be a part of that life."

"But Leroy, I AM a part of that life now, don't you see that? I'm choosing to have a baby with you because I love you and this baby was created in love, but none of that blinds me to what your life is like. Attorney/client privilege aside, I've known you for years, L, and I knew the gamble every time you put that good dick inside me. I accept it baby; I accept it ALL. Now tell me how you're going to keep all you've worked for," she said, putting the plate of half-eaten food down.

For a few seconds I just stared at her, amazed by her compassion and understanding, because they were core attributes that I appreciated beyond words. I reached up and looped my arm behind her neck and pulled her down to me for a kiss.

"Thank you, baby," I said sincerely before letting her neck go.

"You're welcome. Now, what's the plan?"

"Okay, so I've been thinking, and I remembered something I'd heard a long time ago. Before I tell you, though, I need you to understand that rumors in the street about powerful men are nothing new. If it can't be proven in black and white, then it's urban legend, and that's why I gave IG the benefit of doubt for so long. Now I think that was my first mistake. This shit that IG is doing ain't nothing new for him. He used to be a GD, as in a Gangster Disciple—"

"Like a Larry Hoover GD?" she asked.

I was surprised that she knew the name of the founding father, but I let that pass.

"Yeah, that kind of GD. He was under a nigga named Nardo from Richmond, and his ambitions got the best of him because he felt like he should be the head nigga in charge. If I remember my history correctly, this went down about ten years ago. Do you remember hearing about two teenage girls getting executed with shotgun blasts to the face in Richmond?"

"Vaguely. Was that IG?" she asked.

"No, but it was his fault. Back then, no one could get close to Nardo because of his right-hand man named 2. I knew 2 back in the day, and he's a quiet, laid-back nigga, but he's a trained hitta that doesn't hesitate to drop the hammer on anybody."

"His name is 2? You're not talking about a dude from Richmond that raps, from the South side? Real name Henry?" she asked.

"You sound like you know bruh," I said, looking at her closely.

"If that's who you're talking about, then I do. I represented him on a gun case he had, but that was when I first started practicing and I was still with the public defender's office. Now that I think about it though, he is just like you described him, and you can tell by the look in his eyes that he's killed before."

"He has, and his willingness to kill without question or hesitation is part of the reason he was Nardo's second in command. There was no way for IG to gain control of the whole GD movement in Virginia without eliminating 2, but killing him wouldn't work for a few reasons. So IG got creative, just like he's trying to do now with me. He got these two freaked out-ass white girls and sent them to see 2 as a present because his G-Day had just passed. This wasn't out of the ordinary because everybody knew that 2 worked hard enough to deserve playing harder when he had time. Long story short, it was a night of epic proportions that would've made a porn star blush. The two girls took turns with him, and they filmed the whole thing because 2 was cool with it. Turns out those girls were only 14 years old, and he was on the verge of being 19 years old. The tape mysteriously got sent to the girls' parents, and they didn't hesitate to go to the cops. It was all a setup, but it was perfectly executed, so 2 went to prison. IG expected Nardo to turn on 2 and kill him because any sexual crime goes against GD rules, but that didn't happen. Nardo ordered the torture of those girls and their families, at 2's request, until the truth came out. By the time IG got word that Nardo and the whole GD nation was after him, he'd already vanished like smoke. As they say in the movie John Wick, IG became ex-communicado," I said.

"So why didn't Nardo or 2 just kill him after shit died down a little? They could've set him up somehow, I'm sure."

"As fate, or misfortune, would have it, Nardo got locked up with 2 under a RICO indictment. Of course, it was alleged that IG got that ball rolling because if he couldn't have the GD nation, then he'd destroy it," I replied, shaking my head.

"Okay, so how does this help us now?" she asked, looking confused.

"Because no nation is so easily destroyed. They simply go underground. Remember, the greatest trick the devil ever pulled was convincing the world that he doesn't exist," I replied, smiling.

"Nardo and 2 are still running shit?"

"They are. It took time and money to beat the indictment, and 2 still had to serve a few years for the shit with the girls, but they did what they had to do. They've quietly gotten stronger and they're more powerful now than ever, but they never settled the score with IG," I said.

"Ohhhh...so, is the enemy of my enemy my friend, or my enemy? Right?"

"Exactly, and they're my friends," I said, already envisioning the plan coming together.

"And just like that, you have another army at your fingertips. Let the games begin."

# CHAPTER 5

*Lia*

*Los Angeles, California*

"Are we drinking?" Kali asked.

"That's up to you, but it's only 10 a.m., so I'm not trying to get fucked up," I replied.

"Yeah, yeah, you say that shit all the time, bitch. Just go make sure our cabana is fully stocked with the essentials," she said, heading for the floating bar in the middle of the pool.

For a second, I just watched her wade into the shallow end of the rooftop pool while I reflected on my life at this moment. I'd thought that adjusting to yacht life was gonna be crazy before that plan abruptly changed, but living in the penthouse of a hotel in California surrounded by good women, weed, and weather let me into the world Kendrick Lamar rapped about. It was mind-blowing! The fact that Kali and I spent our days laying out in a cabana poolside on top of the Beverly Hills Hilton had a bitch feeling like an heiress. I'd pushed back against Kali's idea for how we should spend our time hiding out for just that reason: because I wasn't nobody's heiress, nor was I a bitch who ducked smoke. Muthafuckas wanted me dead, and the feeling was more than mutual at this point. Kali said she understood my pain and my anger, more so because the callousness of ordering my death had been passed down from her own mother to her. Us becoming allies and forming a unique friendship was not something that either of us had seen or anticipated, but the past month had been wild as a muthafucka, to say the least. Her decision not to kill me, but befriend me instead, was just the beginning. My father getting shot happened right after that, and his blood being shed had me screaming for WAR, not vacation. However, there was a reason my father seemingly trusted Erin above all else with protecting his life.

Even though I didn't know the reason for that, I knew it had to be the reason I listened to her about running instead of fighting to the death. It hurt me to my heart to leave him lying in a hospital bed, which still surprised me because for the last six years, I'd given no fucks about Leroy Bly. He could've died during that timeframe, and I probably would've celebrated, because he deserved worse for murdering his other daughter in cold blood. My sister Cyn.

I was able to understand now why he'd killed her, but the pain of losing her was still fresh in my heart. I still hadn't forgiven him for it, but in the last couple of months, our relationship had taken an unexpected turn into some type of civility on both our parts. Looking back, I couldn't exactly pinpoint when or why things changed, and my own cold heart began to thaw towards my father, but by the time Kali had kidnapped me on her mother's orders, I actually cared about him. The way that he put his life on the line by meeting with Kali alone to get me back showed that he cared about me too. Even though we'd been apart since the meeting of the minds between me, him, and Kali, my feelings had continued to grow, which made me feel like they were out of my control. I wasn't ready to face that fear, so the distractions of living life lavishly on the run was a convenient escape that I'd learned to embrace.

Heading towards our private cabana now, I wondered what type of wild shit I'd see on this day. I'd had so many what-the-fuck moments in the few weeks that we'd been here that I lost count for real. Seeing all the celebrities walk around like normal people was foreign as fuck! For like the first week, I'd forgotten the fact that we were supposed to be hiding out, because a bitch was starstruck every time I turned my head. The day that I'd been standing no more than three feet away from Kendall and Kylie Jenner scantily clad in their bathing suits was my official death date, and I went with a muthafuckin' smile! By now though I was getting used to seeing Hollywood's A-list stars out and about, and I understood that they were just like us regular-ass people, for real. Thanks to Erin giving me unrestricted access to my father's money, I was afforded everything I needed to appear regular to them too. I was still getting used to walking around in a Gucci bathing suit, flaunting the curves my mama had passed on to me. I damn sure wasn't used to getting hit on by women AND men in equal measure for my body's beauty, but I curved all that attention immediately. Kali did too, but it honestly wasn't hard because we'd already admitted to ourselves that we made a cute-ass couple. She was short and beautiful with long blond hair and a body that shouldn't have come with an ass that phat. Despite my tendency to dress masculine like the male role I played in my relationships, I was still 5'7" with a stallion's thickness, and I had that brown-skinned beauty that required no makeup.

Kali and I were definitely attracted to each other too. Even though we hadn't done so much as kiss in all our time together, it was still nice to be around her, and I knew she felt the same way. Despite the intensity of our first meeting, there was no pressure to any facet of our relationship, not even with the threat of death around every corner.

When I stepped into the cabana, I spotted the bronze five-foot-tall hookah pipe standing in the middle of the room, and there were a dozen different containers full of different strains of good weed on the table. We'd been in L.A. for three weeks now and hadn't smoked the same strain of weed twice because there were just so many to choose from and sample. With nothing else to do, we were quickly on our way to becoming marijuana connoisseurs, and we'd even discussed going into business once life looked something like normal.

"Good morning, Ms. Hawkins, would you like something to eat?" Howard asked from behind me.

I turned around to find the cabana's entrance completely blocked by the broad shoulders and shirtless chest of one of our security personnel.

"No thank you, I'm good, Howard."

"Okay, everything that you requested is in here, and just let one of us know if you need anything else. As usual, we have a six-man team up here covering the rooftop, and the rush order that you were expecting has arrived," he said, passing me a wooden box the size that fine Cuban cigars come in.

"Thank you, Howard," I replied, accepting the box from him and setting it on the table.

"If you need me, I'll be right out front."

I waited for him to leave before I sat down on the comfortable lounge chair and opened the box in front of me. The way the sunlight slanted off the polished chrome was a thing of beauty that gave me chills. I lifted the limited-edition Ruger P210 .45 caliber pistol from its foam casing with all the love and tenderness of a mother with her newborn, inspecting it carefully for imperfections. There were two clips in the box, fully loaded, and a third one was already inside the gun. When I ejected the clip from the gun, I immediately noticed the new bullets that I was told to expect when my father had told me about his latest investment. I slid one of the bullets out of the clip before resting the gun and clip in my lap so that I could inspect it closer. The bullet looked smaller than the average .45 round, and it felt lighter in my palm. It wasn't made of traditional metals, but instead some type of poly-alloy combination that wasn't accessible to anyone without a specific military clearance. It was a hollow point capable of piercing a tank's armor, and it packed the punch of a .50 caliber machine gun round, but there was one unique feature of this bullet that I was excited to see. According to my dad's gun connect, when the bullet came into contact with blood, it began to dissolve within seconds, until there was nothing left except for the damage it had caused. The chemicals that were combined to create this dissolving ability also caused a lingering fatal infection that survived in the bloodstream of whoever got hit by the shot. This allowed you take out multiple targets with one shot.

The snipers in the military had named the bullet CANNIBAL. When my father had told me about it a few days ago, I'd thought the shit he was saying was some ole science fiction, Marvel comics type bullshit. That's when he offered to send me what he called a “working sample”, which came with instructions for me to let him know what I thought. The gun enthusiast inside me couldn't WAIT to get my hands on this gun, so I'd asked for it to be specially delivered. Now all I needed was fuck niggas to give me a reason to go apeshit.

"Is that your dad's early birthday present?" Kali asked, coming into the cabana.

"It sure is. Ain't she gorgeous?” I asked, holding up the pistol itself.

She set the bottle of Ace of Spades and the champagne flutes down next to the weed and held her hand out for the pistol. After popping the bullet back into the clip and pushing the clip back into the butt of the gun, I handed it over. I'd already told her about the ammunition, but she was just as curious to see it in action as I was.

"The gun is light," she said, balancing it in the middle of her palm.

"Yeah, I thought so too, and I think its because of the bullets."

"Yeah, it’s that, but I think parts of the actual gun are manufactured from the same alloy as those bullets. Did you notice the trigger though?" she asked, clearly impressed with it.

"Of course. A binary trigger is NOT standard issue, and it makes this piece a sexy muthafucka. To be able to squeeze the trigger, shoot a round, AND shoot a round when you let the trigger go makes this bitch damn near automatic. Sixteen bullets in each clip will get the job done, but can you imagine the beautiful chaos of an extended clip, or a fucking drum on this bitch?"

"Oh God, this is the best foreplay I've had in years! Talk that talk to me, baby," she replied in a sultry whisper while caressing the gun lovingly.

I laughed at the expression of pure delight on her face, knowing that it probably matched my own. Our love for guns and weed were just some of the things we had in common, and the more I learned about her, the more I wanted to know. It was so easy talking to her that we'd somehow got onto the topic of Imani from time to time. I wasn't over her death, but being able to discuss the love and life I'd had with the woman I'd chosen as my future wife, before she was murdered, was helping to heal. Kali understood my pain in a way that told me she knew hurt intimately, but I hadn't pried into her past like the nosy bitch in me wanted to. I did let her know that I was here for her whenever she was ready to talk, so we had that understanding.

"Do you think your dad will send me one too?" Kali asked hopefully, passing me the pistol back.

"I don't know, but I'll ask him. It's to my understanding that the bullets are under mass production for weapons of all calibers, but they only have a handful completed now, and they're not open to the general public. He's been secretly working on this and dumping money into it for the past two years, with only a handful of people knowing."

"That doesn't surprise me in the slightest because I already heard that your father was a man of vision with the ability to play the long game," she replied, reaching for the weed jar labeled BLUEBERRY CHRISTMAS as she moved the hookah.

"I feel like I learn more shit about him with each crisis that comes up because he stays ready for the next move," I admitted, picking up a hose connected to the hookah pipe.

"That's his survival instinct, for sure. I don't know what would make my mom do something do stupid as betraying him, but I honestly don't feel sorry for her. Whatever happens, happens."

"And what if that means he kills her? Can you really live with my father killing your mother?" I asked, searching her deep blue eyes for the truth.

"At first, I couldn't entertain the thought, but now I've analyzed it from every angle, and I know that she brought this on herself. That man gave up EVERYTHING and put it all on the line in the name of love and loyalty. That's almost IMPOSSIBLE to find, and instead of being grateful, my mom was insecure and greedy, so how do fault your dad for whatever happens next? I have to accept it...even if it breaks my heart."

It was easy to see the pain in her eyes, but it was crazy to me how that sadness could transform her beauty into gorgeousness. I didn't doubt her sincerity when it came to her not interfering with my father's decision to handle her mother however he felt necessary, but I knew she'd never be the same. It had been years since I'd lost my own mother in a car accident that wasn't an accident at all, and the pain was still brutal. I missed her every second of every day, and I knew that would've been the case even if her death had been an accident. Knowing that my mother's bitch-ass boyfriend intentionally drove the car they were in into oncoming traffic, causing a head-on collision that ultimately killed her, magnified my pain. Losing someone you loved to unnatural causes hit different, especially when it was the woman who gave birth to you. So, as rational as Kali was being about her mother's death, I knew it was gonna shake her to her foundation. Now that I knew her, had spent time with her and shared laughs with her, I didn't want that pain for her. It wasn't something that she deserved.

"What if we could do something to stop your mom from dying by my dad's hands, or orders?" I asked.

My question froze her movements of packing the pipe with weed as she gave me her undivided attention.

"Do you really think that's possible?"

"I mean, to be honest I don't know. I witnessed my father kill my pregnant sister, and in that moment, I'd never known a more coldblooded, cold-hearted motherfucker walking this earth. Since then, I've learned what really made Leroy pull that trigger that day, and what it ultimately comes down to is him feeling like his own daughter wouldn't stop trying to kill him until she succeeded. In his mind, it was kill or be killed, and looking back at it, I can admit that he was probably right. So all we have to do is take your mom out of that light for him," I replied.

"Okay, but HOW?" she asked, getting visibly excited.

"I don't know, but let's smoke and strategize. I think better high."

# CHAPTER 6

*Leroy*

*2 days later - Atlanta*

"I don't know if she by my side, but the truth is she willing to ride,

Overhead the conversation didn't want it to slide, can you be my soulmate? I'm protecting your pride,

Everything we do together bring confusion and pain, just let me be your rib you will accomplish and gain,

'Cause understanding knowledge is knowing your train, the weight capacity of the money is good when it rains,

On your spare time is all about competition, wanna go handle business while we both reminiscing,

Put the loud in the Dutch smoking on intuition, plus I'm tryna work your mind so I can see your position,

Anniversary is life when it's all a gamble, soon as you make a wish, please blow out the candles,

Gotta avoid burning bridges on the things you handle, like walking on fire with open-toe sandals…"

I watched the man in the booth continue to vibe as the hook to his song came in on cue, and I couldn't help but feel pride. My nigga 2 had long prophesied that he would be one of the greatest rappers to ever put breath on a mic, and now the streets of Atlanta were buzzing with his new single. A lot of times the success of a record could be judged by who wanted to hop on the remix, and from the sounds of the hook playing through the speakers, this particular song had caught Drake's attention. Who would've thought a hood nigga from the south side of Richmond Virginia would be working with the 6 God?

"Ayo, pause the track," 2 said, removing his headphones, and signaling for me to hold up a minute as he came out of the booth.

I took a seat on the couch, grabbed a pre-rolled blunt from the full glass dish on the table in front of me, and lit the torch.

"Muthafuckin' L Boogie! What up, bruh?" 2 asked, coming into the engineering room and flopping down on the couch beside me.

"My nigga 2, the three-headed monster! What's really hood? I see you linked up with Drake on your tender dick shit," I replied, laughing as I passed him the blunt.

"You KNOW I had to do it for the females one time, bruh, and Drake DO THAT SHIT. My next joint got De'rez De'shon on that bitch and it's FIRE!"

"I bet it is, my nigga, I bet it is. I'm proud of you, for real, because you been grinding and putting that work in," I said sincerely.

"I appreciate that, bruh. You know a nigga like me had to take the long way though because I remain loyal to the streets, even now. The money and fame don't mean shit if I ain't a real nigga."

"Facts! But there's a price to pay for being a real nigga, and you gotta keep that in mind. Sometimes the price is too high," I said, accepting the blunt back when he passed it to me.

He looked at me closely for a few seconds, and I knew that he understood my pop-up visit wasn't just a coincidence or to congratulate him. I was the same street nigga he remembered, and I knew he'd see that in my eyes.

"Seems like I've been hearing your name A LOT lately, bruh, so I'm kinda surprised to see you," he said.

"You know that I try to stay a few moves ahead of the storm, and I ain't never nervous, so my composure remains intact."

"I feel that... So what's up though?" he asked, getting down to the reason for my appearance.

"Well, it seems that I've run into a similar situation that you found yourself in once upon a time...with this nigga IG."

Just the mention of this nigga's name caused 2 to laugh softly without humor as he reached for a fresh blunt and lit it. We smoked in silence for a while, but it wasn't strained because I knew what 2 was gonna say. I was prepared for it.

"I TOLD you niggas, bruh, but you didn't wanna listen," he said, shaking his head in obvious disgust.

"It's not that I didn't listen, my nigga. It was that I found out too late in the game. The fact that I've been able to survive his indirect attacks should tell you that I listened to your warning, and I took your advice. I've been making escape plans ever since you put me up on game a few years back when we bumped into each other at bike week in South Carolina. In this situation, I owe my survival to you, fam, but it's deeper than that now. I gotta destroy this nigga or he'll just keep finding ways to fuck real niggas over, and then I'll feel responsible. I need your help to end this shit though."

"What kind of help are you talking about?" he asked.

"The kind that you gotta call Nardo for."

The expression of thoughtful contemplation didn't move from his face, but I saw the change in his eyes when they slid in my direction. Deep down, he'd known as soon as the topic of IG came up that my intentions were all about street politics, loyalty, and that thing inside us with an insatiable thirst. Revenge. Blood would shed in the name of righteousness, but historically, that was nothing new.

"What kind of help are you talking about?" he asked again.

"So right now, IG doesn't know I'm seeing through him, and I'ma keep it like that. I know you've heard shit about my legal troubles, but trust me when I tell you that it ain't as bad as it seems. A lot of smoke without a flicker of flame."

"Smoke can kill you before the flames ever touch you," he stated wisely.

"True indeed, but I'm good over here. What I need to do is find out how many loyalists IG has inside the Nation of Rulers, and I need you to look into his new project, the Camaro Cartel."

"The Camaro Cartel? I think I heard a little something about them niggas because somebody spits bars about them in a YouTube video. I can find out more about them, but it's gonna have to be you who finds out who fucks with this nigga inside your organization. To keep it real with you, I don't think you'll find out who's riding with him until shit gets crazy and muthafuckas start dying. So, are you ready to push all your chips in middle with the info you got?" he asked.

I contemplated the question thoroughly because the answer carried significant ramifications. I knew what would happen if I did nothing, which made waiting it out an impossibility. My only true advantage was the element of surprise, so I had to play the hand I was dealt.

"I'm out of options and short on time at this point. IG has to die in order for me and mine to live, and I'm good with that," I stated calmly.

He nodded his head as he continued to smoke.

"I can pay you whatever outright, or it can be a favor. You choose," I said.

"We'll worry about that later, but for now, I need you to tell me everything I don't know," he said.

"Cool," I replied, lighting a fresh blunt and getting comfortable.

It took me almost an hour and a half to bring him up to speed with all the moving parts to the situation, but once I'd given him the big picture, I could see the wheels and gears clicking behind his eyes.

"One thing about you, bruh. You always keep shit interesting," he said, chuckling.

"It gotta be fun, my nigga, and that brings me to my latest business move that I mentioned briefly."

"The dissolving bullets?" he asked.

I pulled the Ruger P210 .45 from the small of my back, ejected the clip, and passed it to him. He popped a bullet out and looked at it intensely before putting it all back together.

"You down to test out your product?" he asked.

"Without hesitation, my nigga."

He nodded his head before passing the gun back and pulling his phone out of his pocket. His fingers glided across the screen as he composed a text message, and when he was done, he stood up.

"I'll drive," he said, leading the way out of the studio through a side door.

"This muthafucka clean," I said, admiring his 2028 black SRT Hellcat truck.

"I got a blue one too, but Monique driving that one. Anytime I get a new whip, she think she gotta get a matching one, or I gotta let her drive my shit all the time. Crazy!"

"You still with your crazy-ass baby mama Monique? I'm surprised she ain't smoked your ass for EXPLORING your options with other women," I said, laughing as I climbed into the passenger seat.

"Shit, don't think she ain't tried me though. You know that her wild ass is from New York, and psycho is her on her best behavior. When she see how bitches be going for me at my shows, bruh, MANNNNNN, she be HOT!" he replied, laughing with me while starting the truck and pulling off.

"How old is your daughter now, my nigga?"

"Shit, Jaymeka is six years old now and smart as hell. She with my brother Junnie in New York right now because I'm getting ready to hit the road on tour. You already KNOW Monique is gonna be stuck on a nigga hip like a Sig Sauer, so my brother agreed to look out for my baby," he replied.

"If you take the baby on the road, then your baby mama stays busy with her, my nigga."

When he glanced over at me, I could see him thinking about what I'd said, and then he flashed that trademark grin, which signaled his demons at play.

"You right, bruh, you right. Speaking of Monique though, tell me why a nigga had the nerve to rob her when I was out of town last month," he said seriously.

"Word? Who the fuck would be that dumb?"

"Just some Vicki Lou-ass nigga who I put the press on a while back for being on the wrong block flying his flag. I told him that if he knew better, he'd do better...and then the little homies escorted him off the block," he replied, chuckling.

I didn't need to ask what “escort” consisted of because it was obvious the Vice Lord gang member he was referring to had violated and caught an ass whooping for good cause. Going after my man's BM was a bold move. Dumb as fuck, but bold nonetheless.

"Is the nigga still breathing?" I asked.

"He is for now. But that all depends on how good of a shot you are," he said, pulling over in front of a corner store.

When I looked to him in confusion, he nodded his chin towards the three niggas standing outside the store smoking and talking shit to each other in an animated way.

"We good out here, in broad daylight?" I asked, glancing around casually.

"Cameras ain't no issue. You got my word."

"Which one is he?" I asked, pulling my gun out and chambering the first round.

"Since when did you start leaving witnesses?" he countered.

"You're right. You're absolutely the fuck right," I replied, easing the window down.

I glanced around swiftly once again, liking the number of bystanders being none, and I stuck my gun out the window. These niggas were the definition of slipping, and they never saw it coming. I let off eight shots, dropping all three of them, and it didn't feel like I'd pulled the trigger at all.

"PUSSY!" 2 hollered out the window.

After that, all you heard was the Hellcat screaming as we laughed and sped off.

# CHAPTER 7

*Lia*

*Las Vegas, Nevada*

"Are you sure about this, Kali?"

"I am, if you are. I mean it was YOUR brilliant idea!"

"You're right, it was my idea, but in my defense, you KNOW that you was high as fuck," I replied.

"So are you having second thoughts, Lia? Because I can understand if you are."

"Do you two need a minute?" Elvis asked, looking first at me and then at Kali.

Truthfully, we probably needed more than a minute just to process what we were feeling, on top of the millions of renegade thoughts we were having, but time was a luxury that we couldn't afford.

"Loyalty," I said, sticking my hand out towards Kali.

She looked at it for a few seconds and then smiled. "Absolute loyalty," she replied, taking my hand in hers.

"Alright then, I need you both to just repeat after me," Elvis replied, placing his hand on top of both of ours.

We listened closely to him, repeating what he said word for word, and before we knew it, we'd done the unimaginable.

"I now pronounce you wife and wife. You may kiss your bride," Elvis said, lifting his hand off of ours and stepping back.

I hesitated a moment before saying fuck it and pulling her into my arms. The surprise of my actions made her gasp, and me seeing her mouth open gave my tongue a target destination. From the many conversations I'd had with Kali, I knew she was bisexual, but that she'd never actually had sex with a female before. The moment that our tongues started their very enthusiastic exercise of synchronized dancing, my body let me know that this woman was NOT inexperienced when it came to seduction, even if she'd never had a woman melt beneath her touch. The way I kissed her back let her know that I would GLADLY be her first female fatality.

"Wow," she mumbled once we'd pried our lips apart and learned how to breathe independently again.

"I second that notion. Shall we get out of here?"

"Damn right," she replied, interlocking her fingers with mine as we strolled away from the walk-thru wedding chapel.

Rice came flying from somewhere and music followed, but we were in our own world. We didn't let go of each other's hand until we climbed in the backseat of her 2028 Burgundy Rolls Royce Phantom, but as soon as I was seated comfortably behind the window's tint, I found my hand back in hers.

"Did we really just do that?" she asked.

"We definitely did," I replied, pulling the crisp marriage certificate from the pocket of my white low rider Gucci jeans.

When I passed it to her, she smoothed it out in the lap of her white Gucci sundress and simply stared at it for a while.

"Where to?" Howard asked, sliding behind the wheel of the car and starting it.

"Back to Hilton in L.A.," I replied.

We pulled off, but it was clear based on Kali's silence that she was still wrapped up in her thoughts back there with the Elvis impersonator who'd joined us in holy matrimony.

"Are you okay?" I asked after about ten minutes of riding.

"I'm good. I'm just a little shocked, I guess. I imagined my wedding in a lot of different ways, but this is completely different," she replied, smiling at me.

"Yeah, I can understand that. You're an amazing woman though, and I feel lucky to know you, let alone be married to you."

"Awww, your mushy side is so cute," she replied, leaning over and giving me a quick peck on the lips.

"I just want you to know that this ain't just about bringing our families together, even though the idea was birthed from the shit that's going on right now. Getting to know you, laughing and crying with you, and learning from you, has all made me a better woman. There's nothing more that I can ask for in a partner," I said sincerely.

"I agree, and I feel the exact same way about you. Even if this doesn't stop your dad from killing my mom, I still plan to walk through this life with you until you no longer want me to. My pledge of loyalty to you was genuine."

"As is mine, sweetheart. You're my wife, period," I stated, caressing her face gently.

The look in her eyes created a feeling of heat in my stomach that I wanted to explore the long way, but I pushed it down because business had to come first.

"Howard, did you get the wedding ceremony on film like I asked?" I inquired.

"Yes ma'am," he replied, passing me my phone over the seat.

I took a few pictures of the marriage certificate in Kali's lap, and then some of her holding it up and smiling broadly. I passed her the phone so she could get the same kind of pictures of me. Once that was done, I made a quick slide show for all of our social media platforms, and then I uploaded everything.

"We've officially gone public with our marriage, and I'm tagging everyone connected to our parents so it'll be impossible to ignore," I said, tapping away on my phone's screen.

"I'll send it directly to my mom," she replied, pulling out her own phone.

By the time we got to Los Angeles a couple hours later, we'd received big congratulations and well wishes, despite the surprise, but we hadn't heard shit from the main two people we were trying to get through to.

"Has your mom seen your messages yet?"

"Nah, not unless she's checking them from another device, because her iPhone shows it was delivered, but not seen," she replied.

"Okay, well let's forget about it for a while and go do something to take our minds off of everything. We DID just get married. I say we go tour different dispensaries and enjoy the dining experience. I hear there are a few different places that'll let us build our own strain on the spot by combining different blends of marijuana. It's called How High Hibachi. What do you think?" I suggested.

"I'm with that, but I need a shower first, and we need some food."

"Okay. Howard, we're going out in about an hour, so get us an escort please," I said, opening the car door and stepping out.

I kept Kali's hand in mine, and she slid across the seat to exit the car directly behind me.

"Welcome back, Mrs. Hawkins, and congratulations to the both of you," the doorman said, smiling at us as we entered the lobby.

We both murmured our thanks, and then quickly hopped into the elevator and headed for the penthouse. The first thing I noticed when we stepped off the elevator was the waiter standing at our door with a cart full of fruits and sweets and a bottle of champagne chilling on ice. When I looked at Kali, I saw the mischievous glint sparkling in her eyes, which told me that she'd had a hand in the orchestration of this pleasant surprise.

"Good afternoon, ladies, and congratulations."

"Thank you so much. We'll take it from here, and your tip has already been added to this bill," Kali said, quickly inspecting the cart and its contents.

"Very well, ma'am. Thank you and enjoy," the waiter replied, backing away and heading for the now-vacant elevator.

The feeling of appreciation swelled up in my chest swiftly, and I could feel my smile spread across my face as a result. The chocolate-covered strawberries, whipped cream, fresh mango, and assortment of grapes looked appetizing next to the bottle of D'ussé and assorted weed edibles. What I was craving had my mouth watering for a different taste though. I caught her off guard when I literally swept her off her feet, because she was still inventorying the delectables on the cart. I tossed her over my shoulder in a fireman's carry, absorbing her 5'1", 120 pounds with ease as the excitement within me built.

"What are you doing?" she asked, giggling girlishly.

"You're about to find out. Just hold on," I advised.

The cart had been propped against the door, and the door was partially open, so I was able to maneuver us and the food inside the suite without too much difficulty. I scooped up the whipped cream off the cart without breaking stride and handed it to her over my shoulder.

"Wh-what are you——"

"Shhh, I got this," I said, taking her straight to the bedroom. "Do you trust me?" I asked, putting her down on her feet at the foot of the queen-sized bed.

"Of course I do. You know that."

I took the whipped cream from her hands and put it on the bed while slipping my knife from my pocket. With slow, deliberate movements I held the switchblade up at eye level and pressed the button on its side to pop the blade out. Curiosity was alight in her eyes, but it quickly morphed into shock when I took a hold of her dress and slit it down the middle.

"I saw that in a movie once and I always wanted to try it," I said, chuckling softly at the frozen pose she'd assumed.

To her credit, she didn't utter a word or attempt to assert her dominance in any way, and I liked that about her. I slipped the now-ruined garment from her shoulders and proceeded to cut it into strips that would come in handy in the very near future. Once the pile of expensive rags was heaped at her feet, I put the blade in between my teeth and used my hands to help her out of her matching lace turquoise bra and panty set. With the realization of her nakedness and vulnerability made evident by my open staring at her gorgeous body, I watched her blush heat her skin's tone to a warm red shade. This was the first time I'd ever seen her completely nude, and it had been WELL worth the wait. I closed my knife, put it back in my pocket, and quickly shed my own clothing. My nimble fingers hesitated when I got to my black cotton bra and panties, but she was right there to take over. I held my breath as she levelled the playing field, and I fought the urge to flinch or cover up under her intense scrutiny.

"You're beautiful," she whispered, reaching out to lightly run her fingertips over the soft skin from my throat, down in between my breasts.

"Compared to you, I'm just average."

"Don't say that again...because you're beautiful," she insisted, staring up into my eyes.

I could see the flames of desire growing brighter with each passing second, like a beacon calling me home, and that caused my nervousness to flee.

"Lay in the middle of the bed," I instructed.

She moved without hesitation, and that only made my pussy wetter. I had no doubt that if she reached out and touched me right now, I would orgasm and collapse at her feet, forever her slave. I was okay with that, but only when I knew it was a two-way street. I quickly grabbed eight strips of what had been her dress, bound her hands together over her head, and then I used a few more strips to secure her bound hands to the headboard. I had a thought to secure her legs too, but that could wait until later. The last thing I did was grab a piece of her dress and make a blindfold for her eyes to heighten her senses in the moment.

"L-Lia, I've never been…I've never tried—"

"I know, baby, and it's okay. I got you, and I'll go slow...at first," I assured her, positioning her flat on her back with her legs crossed at the ankle.

After going to my carry-on bag in the corner, I returned to the bed with my spur of the moment purchase, a double-sided vibrating strap-on dildo. I knew better than to start with that, so I set it on the bed and picked up the whipped cream as I straddled her.

"Fuck!" she exclaimed, when the first drops of the slightly chilled cream landed on her left nipple.

My chuckle died in my throat because my lips were already locking around her taut, delicate flesh. I started with a little light sucking, which she took in stride, but the simultaneous actions of my tongue dancing with her areola, as my fingers beckoned her closer to satisfaction with their steady motions, made her breath shudder on every exhale. When she inhaled, it almost sounded like she was wheezing, but I wasn't alarmed. More whipped cream was applied, and before she knew it, I had created a NASCAR road course that took me across her breasts, down her smooth stomach, around her belly button twice, until I made my first pit stop at her clit. I watched in fascination as goosebumps rose and fell all over her soft skin following my sucking, licking, and gentle blowing, right before I allowed my teeth to graze her in a sensual nibble. I treated her clit like the first day of summer, and I enjoyed the seconds that built to minutes, exploring it with my tongue and lips. Her pussy was so tight that I could only get two of my small fingers comfortably inside her walls, but her body moved, swayed, and bucked beneath my touch like I had ten fingers pulling the strings of my favorite puppet.

Her first orgasm drowned her within the eighth minute, and her body rocked for the longest 120 seconds of her life in throes of aftershock. Every breath from her mouth sounded like death's gasp and plea for more, so I gave her more. With the taste of whipped cream heavy on my tongue, I made sure to learn her every curve, blemish, scar, and mole until it was all imprinted on the back of my eyelids for eternal viewing. Only after I was convinced that she was mine beyond question did I strap on the flesh-like dildo, slipping half of the 12 inches inside my wet, throbbing pussy, and finally feeding my own hunger. As a giver, I received pleasure from my partner's experience, but Kali was the first woman to ever have me famished and literally craving for her to take me. My only goal now was pushing us into that life after death. I flipped her onto her stomach while climbing on top of her, and grabbed a fistful of her hair as I plowed the thick, vibrating dildo into her hard enough to snatch my own breath away. The feeling of simultaneous fulfillment was beyond description, and it threatened to render me unconscious instantly.

"Ohhhh Lia," she whined, causing the hair on the back of my neck to stand up.

The sounds that came from in between my lips couldn't be classified as human, but I didn't give a fuck because I knew no shame. I only got three strokes in before I came all over my end of the toy, and was left shaking hard enough to chip two teeth. Luckily, she was right there with me, flying through the gates of breathless climax because I was no good after the first one, and I collapsed on the bed beside her. I managed to push her blindfold up so that she could roll over and see me, but I was too weak to untie her. We both got a laugh out of that, as we fought for oxygen to replenish all that our untamable desire had taken away.

"Y-you good?" I asked, working on undoing the knot to release her hands.

"No, I'm SOOOO much better than that."

"Glad I could help," I replied, laughing with pride and satisfaction.

Once her hands were free, she wrapped her arms around my neck and pulled me in for a kiss that defined passion in every language. The way she kissed me created an instant restart to the games I wanted to play with her until time stopped, but there were a couple more surprises in store for her today, so round two would have to wait.

"Let's take a shower, because we still have places to go and things to do," I said, reluctantly pulling back and sitting up.

"Awww, but this is so much more fun," she replied, pouting in a sexy way.

I took her hand in mine, leading her to the shower, where we spent another half an hour learning more fun ways of communicating and multitasking.

"You're my first and I'm your LAST woman, because you got me fucked up if you think I'ma let you fuck another bitch!" she said, laughing as she got dressed.

"I promise that you ain't seen shit yet. It gets soooo much deeper now that we've connected on multiple levels, and the best part is that we're friends too. You're my best friend."

I hadn't meant to get heavy in this moment, but I could tell by the way she stopped and looked at me that what I'd said had touched her.

"You're mine too, sweetheart," she replied, crossing the room to me.

I opened my arms to receive her embrace, but before we could touch, someone banged on the front door to the suite.

"I'll get it. It's probably just—"

"Wait," I said, grabbing her wrist firmly.

I could tell by the look of confusion on her face that I was giving off weird vibes, but my focus was elsewhere.

"That's the police," I whispered.

"What? How do you know that when you can't see through the door, babe? Stop being paranoid."

"Because I'm a cop, and I know what it sounds like when you bang on a door with a Glock .40 in your fist," I said, moving towards my bag so I could grab my guns.

"You're tripping, Lia. Just let me—"

Her words of dismissal were interrupted by the sound of muffled gunshots, which sent my mind reeling backwards to my condo in Richmond.

"Not again."

# CHAPTER 8

*Leroy*
*Atlanta*

"Ayo, you're still the craziest nigga I know, bruh," 2 said with a wide grin on his face.

"That's only because you don't count yourself on that list of crazy muthafuckas," I replied, tucking my still-warm pistol back into the waist of my jeans.

"Either way, niggas in this generation need to be more like us instead of so bitch made. The only time you really hear about a nigga getting active is over some pussy that don't belong to him, and they be thinking that shit is gangsta! How's that gangsta, when that same bitch you going hard for is sucking and fucking your opps before the magistrate can give you a bond?"

"Come on and PREACH then, my brother," I said, chuckling at the animated look on his face.

"Real shit, bruh, niggas got the game fucked up. That shit that just happened back there didn't go down because Monique is some bitch I'm tender dick over. Monique is my daughter's MOM, meaning she family, and that means I'ma ride for shorty FOR LIFE. The real reason shit got ill though is because dude is the opps, and he made a disrespectful declaration of war when he came for mine."

"That's definitely something I can understand, my nigga, and I'm going through the same shit," I replied, shaking my head and thinking about Lia.

"Exactly! That's why I'ma help you, for real. The history that I got with this nigga IG is a factor, but it's not the biggest reason that I'm lending you my resources. It's the right thing to do," he said, looking over at me briefly before putting his eyes back on the road.

We cruised on with just the sounds of T.I. rapping coming from the truck's speakers to fill the silence, but I drew strength from the comradeship. I was the type of nigga who would go to the end of the earth when something made sense, and when it was for me and mine. 2 was the same kind of nigga, cut from the same cloth, and that made his thoughts, feelings, and outlook on shit matter to me. Had he tried to talk me out of all out warfare, I would've at least considered it because he probably was reasoning from an angle that I wasn't looking at. A lesson I'd learned in prison was to ALWAYS seek wise counsel when it came to serious shit, so coming to see 2 wasn't my last stop before I took aim at my enemies. If one head was better than two, then I planned to have more heads than a hydra by the time my opps knew what was coming their way.

"Where we going?" I asked, realizing that we weren't headed back to the studio.

"To link up with my right-hand man, Phantom."

"Oh, a'ight," I replied, leaning back in the seat and getting comfortable.

2 stuck his hand down into the seat's console and pulled out a silver case with a bud leaf and diamonds on it and a matching lighter. He passed both to me. I took a blunt out, lit it, and told my dude to fill me in about this tour he was set to go on. He ran down the crisscross trek that they were getting ready to run from east to west to south to north across America, with it ending in Canada. That lined up perfectly with his tour ending at the same time and place as Drake's OVO (October's Very Own) tour kicking off. which made Drake hopping on the remix to 2's song a perfect business play for both of them.

"I'm proud of you, bruh," I said genuinely.

"Thanks, but wait til you see me do my THING in live concert, nigga. I line up the competition and knock their fucking heads off!"

"No doubt. I'ma pull up on you when you slide through a city I'm in, but I'm calling ahead of time because you

KNOW that me and my team need that backstage treatment, " I said, smiling.

"Say less, bruh. Listen though...you know I wouldn't hesitate to go to war side by side with you if it wasn't for this tour, but—"

"My nigga, chill, because you don't gotta explain that shit to me. It's already understood and solidified when it comes to me and you, so we good. I'd smack the shit out of you if you gave up this tour," I assured him, holding up my fist.

He dapped me up as we hung a right into the parking lot of a warehouse. When we pulled up to the building, I sized it up, and immediately recognized the potential for legit or criminal enterprise to be run from this spot.

"Location, location, location," I said, opening my door and following 2 out of the truck.

"This is one of my nigga Phantom's spots. I knew he was here, so I told him we'd pull up on him so that we could discuss business."

"Lead the way," I replied, invoking a nonchalant calm into my movements despite my hyper vigilance.

When we got to the front door, 2 looked directly into the Ring camera mounted on the locking mechanism, and then he placed his palm on the glass door. The doors were covered with mirror tint from top to bottom which made peeking inside an impossibility, but the dope part was the technology at work. When 2 pulled his palm back, a silhouette of it in green lines remained imprinted on the glass, and you could tell that his palm and fingerprints were being analyzed. A few seconds later, the loud sounds of gears in motion could be heard coming from behind the glass, and then several lock tumblers rolled.

"All is well," an automated voice stated.

Without hesitation, 2 took ahold of the door and pulled it open for us to step through.

"I like that shit right there," I said, looking at the door closely as we walked in.

"Yeah, my nigga takes his security serious, but you'll see why in a second."

The front of the warehouse was set up like the waiting room in a corporate building, equipped with magazines and a filtered water cooler in the corner. 2 led the way past the unmanned receptionist desk, and further into the building down a darkened hallway. When we came to another door like the one out front, he went through same procedure. This time when the door in front of us was open to our access, I got to see what all the security was for. In the wide-open space of the warehouse stood ten identical transparent shipping containers, big enough to hold a full-length conference table in the middle of them, and each equipped with a gorgeous naked female standing in front of each table, working. Each table was full of something illegal and lucrative. There were tables full of a white crystalized powder, multi-colored pills, different strains of marijuana by the pound, explosives, and guns. Within seconds, I realized I was looking at an assembly line that had to be netting millions of dollars a month, depending on production and clientele. Right then, I knew Phantom had earned his name, because a nigga doing business on this scale was one I should've known or heard about.

"Damn, these bitches are BAD," I said, admiring all the naked flesh we were walking past.

"Yeah, and they get better benefits with pay than the strip club, so they're happy to work here."

I followed 2 down the aisle created by the containers on each side until we came to a glass office that contained its own massive desk made of oak, lined with money machines and cash.

"2, what's up, my nigga?" Phantom asked, taking a break from counting long enough to greet his mans officially.

I sized him up immediately in the way hittas do. It was obvious that the suit fitting his slightly muscular frame was tailored, and the Versace frame glasses on his face were just for show. His dreads were neat, freshly twisted, and came down to the top of his chest, which meant he knew how to clean up his hood shit to mingle with the white folks. When I looked into his eyes, though, I got the understanding that I was looking for. In every REAL street nigga, there was a knowledge hidden in their darkness that was identifiable to those who knew that same darkness, almost like finding a lighthouse in the fog. It was easy to see if you knew what you were looking for, and it was impossible to fake because a real nigga would smell forgery like a shark does a drop of blood in the ocean.

"This is my nigga, L Boogie," 2 said, introducing me.

I gave a brief second for Phantom to run the same diagnostic check on me that I'd run on him, but it didn't take long for him to extend his hand.

"What's up, bruh?" Phantom asked.

"Not a whole lot, but I admire your operations," I replied, nodding towards the warehouse floor of activity on display in front of us.

"Appreciate that. This spot us just one of many," Phantom replied nonchalantly.

"And yet, I've never heard of you. I like that," I admitted, smiling.

"I'm sure if the great Leroy Bly asked enough questions, he could find out anything, about anyone," Phantom replied with a wink.

I didn't let the fact that he knew me show on my face in the slightest, especially since I knew it was an opening gambit to catch me off guard. It was cute, kinda like a French open in chess when you see it for the first time.

"True, but I don't ask questions unless they're necessary. In this situation, my man 2 assured me that questions ain't necessary," I replied.

He nodded in understanding before taking a step back so that he was positioned in front of me and 2 together.

"So what brings you niggas to my humble abode?" Phantom asked.

2 looked at me and gave me a slight nod, which I took as my cue to run everything down. I gave Phantom the Cliff Notes version, because the importance for him would lie in the future, not the past. When I was done speaking, he looked at 2, who issued another slight nod, and then he proceeded to go around his desk to his phone. He made a call that lasted five minutes, and despite me being right there, I didn't understand a word of what he said because it was in a code spoken fluently by him and the person on the other end. I caught the smirk on 2's face though, and that told me that he understood every muthafuckin' word. When his call was done, he returned back to his position in front of me and 2.

"Whenever, wherever, all you gotta do is call and we're there to bring death. My people are already working on these Camaro Cartel niggas because they was trying to get in the way of business that didn't concern them. We gon' knock the Chevy emblem off their shit. As for the Nation of Rulers, it's like bruh told you, you're gonna have to figure that out. Personally, I believe that if you kill IG and Zuk, no one will DARE fuck with you, but as long as they're alive, you're looking at a house divided. I don't have to tell you how dangerous that is. Like I said though, you got all of our hittas at your disposal, but that DOES come with a price on my end."

"What's the price?" I asked readily.

"Nothing that you saw on any of those tables you walked past equates to the drug you supply. Nothing comes close to FUTURE, so for this favor that you're asking, I'm asking for a steady supply of FUTURE," Phantom replied.

"I can do that, and I'll do you one better. I'm gonna give you access to one metric ton of product as bait to lure IG out into whatever trap you wanna set for him. I'm gonna give you the location and the codes to get in to one of our warehouse operations. All you gotta do is hit the location and use a little misdirection by flying the Camaro Cartel flag. You keep what you kill in terms of whatever you find in that warehouse, but I personally guarantee nothing under a metric ton of FUTURE," I said.

I could tell that Phantom was trying to play it cool, but we all understood how much money I was offering up by way of some top-notch product. My shit was upper echelon, meaning you could cut it enough to turn one into two without losing a single client to your competition. This was a deal no one could refuse - not even Vito Corleone.

"Well, that's definitely a way to start a war, and I'm with it," Phantom said.

"Cool. Then let's get down to the details, because I've gotta head back up North to move the next chess piece."

# CHAPTER 9

*Lia*

"Take this, and no matter what happens, stay behind me," I said, passing Kali my Ruger P210 .45 with both extra clips.

After she was armed, I dug in my bag for my collapsible AR-15 carbine with the two 50 round drums that accessorized this nasty muthafucka. My eyes stayed glued to the door as my fingers flew on autopilot, readying the gun for dinner and dessert. I shoved a drum in each of my pants pockets, and then I made sure to flip the safety off my gun.

"We can't stay here," Kali whispered, tugging on my arm.

My ears were tuned to the sounds of movement coming from outside of our hotel room door, but what she said still registered, and I knew she was right. In this moment, I didn't know whether to thank God or Leroy Bly, because his money had given us an escape route right now.

"Come on," I whispered, making a mad dash out of the bedroom, across the living room, and into the built-in kitchen area.

In the last five years, robberies and home invasions against the 1%er's of the world had become such a lucrative racket for criminals that the rich people had to stay a step ahead of them. That meant installing more panic rooms in homes that were nuclear bomb proof, and for hotels, that meant developing fast-acting escape plans that worked with the precision of pulling a fire alarm. One of the best-selling points for the patrons of the Hilton Beverly Hills penthouses was the secret, private elevators. It had taken a $100 million dollar renovation to install twelve escape elevators throughout the massive hotel, but the peace of mind it afforded its guests for this extra precaution was priceless. The elevators weren't a part of the old or new blueprints, and they were all built to let their passengers off at a designated security station. The manager of the hotel had personally come to show me and Kali where our elevator was located, and had even given us a test run. Right now, I could kiss that man in the mouth for that.

As soon as we entered the kitchen area, I went for the pantry and pulled the fire alarm handle by the door. This set off a silent alarm that would send the building into lockdown protocol - but not before opening the hidden door built into the wall of the pantry. Just as the door opened, I heard gunfire blow the key card lock off the penthouse's front door, forcing more adrenaline into my veins. I pulled Kali in behind me, shut the door, and hit the only button on the panel, which signaled immediate distress. Less than a second later, we were descending at rapid speed, but I still wasn't feeling the comfort of safety.

"Keep the gun at your side, babe, so we don't get shot by mistake," Kali said, taking my free hand into hers.

I did what she said and let the barrel of the AR-15 rest against my leg. It didn't escape my notice how much calmer her presence made me feel. Her grip was firm on mine, and her palms weren't moist, which checked my own body's reactions somehow. When I looked over at her, she gave me a wink and a smile, which forced me to crack a grin. I didn't know how anyone could be this cool in the face of a direct attack, but I definitely appreciated her calm keeping my panic in check for the moment. Outwardly, I could tell by my reflection off of the elevators paneling that I looked unfazed, but inside, I was hearing Imani's screams, and that shit had my soul rattled.

The elevator came to a complete stop, and I shuffled my feet in anticipation of the door opening while releasing some of the nervous energy bottled up. When the door didn't open, though, I felt my anxiety ratchet up a thousand notches. A sudden jerking motion from the elevator had me raising my gun again to shoulder level. Instead of letting my hand go so that I could get a good grip on the gun, Kali squeezed my hand tighter.

"Baby, wait, do you feel that? The elevator is moving sideways, left to right instead of up and down, and the manager told us why that would happen. Remember?" she asked gently.

It took me a few deep breaths to get my brain to unscramble, but eventually it did, and I could hear the managers voice in my mind clearly.

"He told us that all escape elevators went to security stations, just not the same ones. He also said that the door to the elevator wouldn't open if that particular security station wasn't secure, and the elevator's programming would reroute it to another security station," I replied.

"That's right, babe. And what happens if the next station isn't secure?"

"We go into a secure panic room that's beneath the hotel," I replied, feeling slightly claustrophobic at the thought of having a building sitting on top of me.

"So it’s all good, and I'm right here with you. We're okay."

Nothing in my life has ever felt better than the heat of her palm against my own in that moment, and I focused all my energy on that while continuing to regulate my breathing. The elevator abruptly came to its second stop, but this time, there was no delay with the elevator doors opening, and I experienced the joy the disbelievers must've felt when Moses parted the Red Sea. Before either of us could take a step forward, though, two mean looking 12-gauge semi-auto Bullpop shotguns greeted us.

"Hands up, and drop the weapons."

We both did as we were told, moving with deliberately slow and exaggerated movements because there was no doubt that one blast from either gun would make cleanup a BITCH for housekeeping.

"State your name and security clearance number," a tall black man demanded.

"Hawkins, number 556961," I replied.

A few seconds later, I heard an automated voice echo.

"Identity confirmed, facial recognition confirmed."

This made the two men in front of us lower their weapons and take a refreshing step back, which gave the short, sexy Latina woman room to step forward.

"Mrs. Hawkins, please accept our apology on behalf of the Hilton Beverly Hills. Would you please gather your weapons and follow me?" she requested politely.

We did as she asked, and we were led out of the elevator, down a short hallway where we came to a stairway, and then up one flight of steps. Normally I'd expect to see some writing on the wall alerting me to what floor we were on, but there were no markings on these white walls. There were no visible cameras either. When we came out of the stairway, we stepped into a hallway that locked identical to the penthouses that we'd just escaped, and for a moment, I felt the icicles of fear forming in my chest.

"Where are we going?" I asked, squeezing Kali's hand to send her the message of unease.

"To a suite that technically doesn't exist, until you can safely exit the hotel."

"Who are you exactly?" Kali asked.

This question made the woman in front of us stop walking so that she could turn and face us, which halted our forward progression as well.

"Names aren't important, but let's just say that I'm with hotel management, and I mean you no harm. My job at this moment is to make sure you both stay alive so that you can leave a five-star review for our EXTRA special services. My plan is to escort you into the suite at the end of the hall here and give you access to a laptop and phone so that you can make the necessary moves to protect yourselves. The premium that you paid when you reserved your suite is what affords you this treatment. In addition, I will help you in any other ways that I can, within reason, but I cannot kill for you."

"Ah, so that's where you draw the line?" I asked sarcastically.

"Yes, Mrs. Hawkins, that is the line I will not cross. But not because I'm scared. I simply believe in each individual putting their own work in," she replied before turning and continuing to lead us up the hallway.

Kali and I exchanged a glance that came with smiles of respect as we followed our escort with our hands still clasped tightly together.

"Is there anything else that you require?" she asked once she had us set up with everything she'd promised in the suite.

"Yeah. I wanna see the footage of the attack against us from the hotel hallway's angles," I replied.

"Not a problem," she said, turning the laptop that was sitting in front of me on the table towards her.

A few seconds and half a dozen keystrokes later, she spun the laptop back to me before walking from the room.

"Babe, I need to sync my ghost thumb drive from out of the cloud, so you're gonna have to be on the laptop searching anything you think we need," I said.

"Ghost thumb drive? What the hell is that?"

"It's just what it sounds like, but it's an app. With this app, I can sync my phone to any electronic device and dump the contents onto a thumb drive that forever stays in the cloud, encrypted. It only takes a few minutes, but due to only having the standard gigabytes of a thumb drive, we have to be selective about what we're downloading," I replied.

"I ain't never heard of no shit like this, Lia, so where did you get it?"

"One of the perks of being a cop. It's still in its infancy stage of development, which means its illegal as fuck," I admitted, pulling my phone out.

All she could do was shake her head, but she moved the laptop in front of her so that she could type. Once I accessed the app, I gave her the nod, and together, we went through footage that the hotel had to offer. Seeing what happened was the goal, but also seeing how it had happened and what stuck out in the last 24-36 hours leading up to it. I wasn't watching the laptop because I was watching my phone to make sure the app was working, but the moment I heard Kali murmur "oh fuck", my eyes and mind shifted focus.

"What is it?" I asked.

"You were right, babe. Look," she replied, rolling the footage back a little before letting it play again.

At first, nobody was in the hallway except for Howard and one of his security coworkers, but they were both distracted by the big butt white girls in maid uniforms as soon as they appeared. They chatted with them for a few minutes, and then the show began. All of a sudden, a cop in uniform stepped out of the stairway and checked the situation out with one curious-eyed sweep of the hallway. Howard and his buddy were as clueless as the two females, who were laughing just a little too hard at whatever joke they were hearing. The cop strolled up on them and startled the women, who put their hands up out of reflex or flirtation. The cop motioned for them to put their hands down, and then they all started to engage in a conversation. Seeing all of this had me annoyed as FUCK because there was no audio to go with the video, but I pushed that aside so that I could focus on the body language.

"Do you think the cop knows the maids?" Kali asked.

"It smells like a setup from here, so I'm thinking he probably does. The cop seems vaguely familiar though, so maybe he just hangs around the hotel in plainclothes."

The conversation with the cop, the maids, and our security detail continued for a few more minutes, but the moment the second cop stepped out of the stairway, the energy did a dramatic shift. The second cop's strides were purposeful, and his hand was on the butt of his gun from the first frame of him on screen. He was all business. As he neared the group, the maids stepped back ever so slightly, which created the vulnerability to Howard and his sidekick that confirmed my suspicions of a setup. The first cop drew his gun because nobody was paying attention to him, and before Howard knew it, he was feeling the cold steel of a Springfield 1911 9mm pistol pressed to the soft skin behind his right ear. The second cop pulled a two-tone Glock .19 with a suppressor on the end and rested it calmly in between the eyes of our second security person. The maids vanished calmly, like empty rain clouds. Howard was laid on the floor, and then the first cop started banging on our hotel room door.

"I can't believe you knew it was a cop just from the knock, babe," Kali said, fascinated and shaking her head.

"Just a cop thing. I've been the one doing the banging enough times to know that sound in my sleep."

The cop in the video banged a few more times, and that's when he made his move. He lunged at the feet and ankles of the first cop, which resulted in him getting back handed viciously. The second cop decided to keep his hands clean in a literal sense, so he pulled the trigger and pushed the guy's brains out through the back of his skull. From there, he swiftly turned his gun on Howard, and before the first cop could intervene, the second cop shot Howard twice in the head. From that point, an argument between the cops ensued, but it was brief because both of them quickly remembered why they were there to begin with. It wasn't until the first cop went back to banging on the door of our suite that I saw something in him that made my stomach drop.

"Oh fuck," I mumbled, looking over at Kali.

I expected her to be nodding her head in obvious agreement, but the expression contorting her features now was one of confusion.

"Why do I feel like we're not on the same page?" I asked.

"Me too. Why did you say 'oh fuck'? I thought it was because the fucking LAPD is on camera, trying to hunt us the fuck down like we're Taliban terrorists," Kali replied, clearly pissed off, but still confused.

"I said oh fuck because I realized who the first cop is, and why he looked familiar to me." She looked at the laptop's screen long enough for it to be considered staring, but when she looked back at me, it was still with confusion.

"Baby, you really don't see it?" I asked.

"No. Who is he?"

"He's the same muthafucka you hired, Kali. The same muthafucka who was gonna kill me on that airplane."

# CHAPTER 10

*Leroy*

"Where the fuck are you, and why you ain't been answering your phone, Leroy?"

I could tell by her tone of voice that all the sweet talking I'd been practicing in my mind, since I saw the amount of missed calls I had from her, was useless. She was one pissed bitch right now, and being pregnant only enhanced the fire-breathing monster in her.

"Baby, I told you that I'd be in Atlanta on business for a few days, and for you not to panic if you didn't hear from me sometimes. You've got my phone low-jacked, so you know EXACTLY where I am," I replied, trying to use the rational and patient approach.

"Fuck ALL that shit you're talking 'bout right now, because we had an understanding that you would check in with me on a regular basis! Otherwise I would've sent Benji, Malikye, and a hundred muthafuckas like them with you, so stop playing with me," Erin growled through clenched teeth.

"You're right, sweetheart, and I apologize for not sticking to the agreement. I won't make excuses. Is everything okay up there?"

For a few seconds she didn't respond, but I could still heart her harsh, angry breathing clearly over the open phone line.

"Everything is NOT okay, and there's no way it could be. The baby is fine, but my soon-to-be ex-husband has decided to be a dick about letting me see my boys right now. He doesn't know exactly what's going on, but someone has been whispering in his ear that my life is too dangerous all of a sudden. It's bullshit!"

"Okay, just breathe, baby. I promise that I'll go have a friendly talk with him when I get back," I reassured her.

"I AM breathing, Leroy, and no you WON'T talk to him, because you've got other shit to deal with and worry about. I can handle little dick Daniel. I just didn't want the drama to start, but it's feeling unavoidable at this point."

"We're a team, Erin, which means we handle our problems TOGETHER. Plus, you know that we work better together," I said softly, hoping to ease the tension humming over the phone line.

I heard her chuckle briefly, and then take a much-needed deep breath.

"Only YOU would pick now as a time to flirt and throw out sexual innuendo, like I don't miss that dick putting me to sleep at night too. You're right though, we do work better together. But it hasn't felt like TOGETHER since you left. I just...I miss you," she confessed vulnerably.

"Awww, I miss you too, babe, and I mean that. I saw ten naked women a little while ago, and sex didn't even cross my mind."

"It better not have, or I'll cut your fucking dick off!" she blurted out.

Despite the seriousness of the threat, I laughed heartily because her outburst only proved how fucked up she was about me.

"I'm sorry, L, it's just hormones on top of EVERYTHING else is making me crazy with capital letters. I'm surprised you're not more unsettled and anxious considering Kali and Lia's latest stunt, but it's good that you––"

"Wait, wait, wait, hold up. What are you talking about? What did Kali and Lia do?" I asked.

"You haven't been on social media, babe? Oh wow."

"If I didn't have time to check in on YOU, what makes you think I'd have time for some damn social media? I don't live on social media like today's generation, so please tell me what the fuck happened," I said with growing irritation.

"You don't gotta bite MY fucking head off! Jesus. All they did was get married."

"What? Who got married?" I asked, confused.

"Kali and Lia got married in Las Vegas."

"They got married to WHO? And why the fuck would they pick NOW to bring new people into our dysfunctional-ass family?" I asked, feeling my irritation about to hit its boiling point.

"Leroy, you're not LISTENING, baby. They didn't bring nobody new into the family. They married EACH OTHER," she replied slowly.

In an instant, my head felt like one of those old Jet Blue airline commercials where the information being given literally made the person's head pop off and blow away like colorful pixie dust powder in the wind. I was too stunned to talk, and I could tell by the expression on my nigga 2's face that my mouth was sitting in my lap. My mind kept trying to arrange the pieces of the puzzle that showed Kali and Lia getting married, but from no angle did those pieces fit. The shit didn't make sense! I was old enough and mature enough to know that love just didn't make sense sometimes, but this situation didn't feel like that. This shit felt like a strategic move, but the hand moving these pieces was unseen by me.

"Where are they now?" I asked, fighting for calm.

"As far as I know, they're back in L.A., living like pampered princesses."

My instincts told me to hop on a red eye flight and show up at their fucking hotel room door, but that moved tasted irrational on my tongue and so I had to swallow it. What I needed to do was let this information have free reign over the amusement park that was my mind, and that way it could be processed properly.

"I'm on my way to you now. Sit tight," I said, disconnecting the call before she could respond.

"Everything good, bruh?" 2 asked.

"Just more drama, which means I've gotta go. I'll be in touch though, my nigga, and tell Phantom I said to be ready," I said, dapping him up as I got up off the studio couch.

We'd come back here and got caught up in a private listening party after the meet and greet with Phantom. I'd meant to get back on the road sooner, but the vibe of good music and weed kept me stuck in the moment. Now it was time to get back to the mayhem. I hopped on my 2028 blood red Ducati 916R sports bike, feeling the excitement building in my veins because I was about to unleash one of the fastest street bikes in the world. On the drive down to Atlanta, I'd only got the bike up to 204 mph, and that bitch hadn't shaken in the slightest. More could be demanded from this machine though because the speedometer registered the top speed as 250 mph, but I'd personally been told that 265 mph was the limit between brilliance and insanity. I was ready to find out for myself.

As I navigated through downtown Atlanta, I kept my speed conservative, but the moment I hit the outskirts of the city, I let that muthafucka EAT! In under seven seconds, I was riding the wind at 180 mph, and from there, all it took was a slight flick of the wrist to see 200 mph glowing in green LED lights. I ran most of the way to Virginia between 195-205 mph, but when I found myself on a familiar straight shot stretch of I-95, I decided to run with the gods. At 250 mph it felt like I was flying, but still I demanded more by twisting the throttle all the way back. The moment that I saw the 265-mph glowing at me through the darkness, I felt invincible, and I allowed myself a full ten seconds like that before I broke it back down to 200 mph. The drive from Atlanta to Richmond took two hours and thirteen minutes.

I parked my bike beside the side gate to Erin's gated community that she used to share with her husband, and then I snuck on to the property on foot. The only lights on in Daniel's house were those in the living room, and when I peeked through the window, I saw him passed out on a recliner in front of the TV. I waited a few seconds, searching every inch of the room that my eyes could reach, until I was certain that neither of Erin's sons was in harm's way. After that, I crept to the garage door and forced open the side door leading into the house as quietly as possible. On tiptoe, I made my way to the living room, pulled my gun out slowly, and held it inches from his right eye.

"If you scream, you die," I vowed in a deadly whisper.

Daniel's eyes popped open and immediately locked on the barrel that was threatening to alter his line of sight and breathing patterns.

"Wh-what do you want?"

"For you not to be a dick, Daniel, that's all. At one point you loved Erin and you were happy together, but that time has passed now. Let it go, because I promise you, if you choose to make her or these kids suffer in ANY way, I'll kill your entire family, and save you for last. You may not know me, Daniel, but my reputation speaks for itself, and it was well-earned. I won't just kill you either. I'll BREAK you. I'll torture each and every person you love until you put a gun in your mouth and pull the trigger just to save me the trouble. There's nowhere you can hide from me, and no one can keep you safe from my reach. Give Erin whatever she asks for in the divorce, and never, EVER, use your kids as pawns against her again. That'll get you killed too," I warned.

"And what if I say fuck you, and fuck that trifling, two-timing whore? What are you gonna do then, BOY? Because I sure as hell ain't scared of you. I've got friends that kill you fake gangsters for sport and mount your heads as trophies."

He was talking tough, and the way he said the word “boy” sounded too much like “nigger”, but I could tell by the look in his eyes that his bravado was hollow. I could taste the desire to shoot him coating my mouth and riding my tongue like Erin's last kiss. I didn't do it though, because the trauma of their sons finding their father dead was something I didn't wanna inflict on them. There was another way to call his bluff without killing him right now, and it started with me lowering my gun to my side.

"Do you know who I am, Daniel?"

For a second, the confusion over me moving my pistol away from his face was blocking the necessary receptors for his common sense, but he recovered swiftly.

"Am I supposed to know you muthafucka?" he sneered.

"Well, in case you thought I was just some guy who stole your motorcycle, let me formally introduce myself. My name is Leroy Bly, businessman, philanthropist, and Supreme Ruler in the Nation of Rulers motorcycle club. You may have seen my face on TV for the levelling of that women's prison not long ago. In case you don't know who the Nation of Rulers are, well, I suggest you go ask those 'friends' of yours. And then you'll understand that my words aren't threats. They're promises. Your sisters and parents all live in towns within an hour of this location, so would you rather I kill them to make my point?"

The defiance in his eyes almost resulted in him spewing some more slick shit out of his mouth, but I'd seen his eyes get wider with recognition when I spoke about knocking the prison into dust and dead bodies. He thought better of his comments, and kept his lips pressed together.

"If you see me again, you die. If you disrespect Erin, you die. If you understand, then just nod your head," I stated.

Once he complied, I spun my pistol around and cracked him over the head with it fast and hard, leaving him slumped unconscious in his recliner. As quietly as I came, I left, and was back on my bike in the wind five minutes later. Part of me wanted to pull over for the night and rest, but I wanted to be with Erin even more, and that's what I focused on as Kentucky became my destination.

It was another two hours and twenty minutes before I was bringing my bike to a stop outside of Dana's cabin, where I was met with sleep-deprived eyes and automatic weapons.

"Mr. Hawkins, we weren't expecting you tonight, sir. We'd thought you'd gone straight to L.A.," Benji said, stepping out of the shadows a few feet away from the cabin's front door.

"Well, surprise. Where's Erin?" I asked, already hopping off the bike and moving towards the cabin.

"She's—"

Before Benji could answer my question fully, the door to the cabin was flung open, and Erin came bolting through it at a dead run. As soon as her feet reached the edge of the wooden porch, she took to the air in the graceful leap she'd mastered in her ballerina days. I was there to catch her and pull her to my body like she was the truest extension of the beating heart in my chest and I needed her.

"I missed you too," I said, holding her close.

"Oh God, L, I was so worried about you. I kept calling and calling you, and when you didn't answer, all that I could do was pray you were on your way."

"Baby, I told you I was coming to you, so why were you worried? " I asked, putting her down on her feet so that I could look down into her eyes.

"Because I thought you'd got word about Kali and Lia being attacked at their hotel in L.A. by someone posing as LAPD. I didn't want you to go out there and take on the whole LAPD trying to find rogue cops," she replied.

I had to quiet the screaming in my head that had started the moment she said someone had attacked my daughter, so I didn't speak for a few seconds.

"I didn't know Lia and Kali were attacked until you just told me, but now I AM going out there," I said.

"There's no point in that, because Lia and Kali ain't there," she replied quickly.

"Where are they?" I asked, fighting the panic that was clawing at my throat.

"They think Gini is behind the attack, so they went after her to convince her to stop, or kill her if she won't."

# CHAPTER 11

*Lia*

*2 days later - Roanoke, Virginia*

"Of all the places your mom could go to, what makes you think she'd be here?" I asked.

"Because she can't access her money without me, which means she needs to regroup and think. The only place she would feel safe is the city she grew up in, and the cops ain't looking for her because they think she'd dead. My grandmother on her side is still here, and so is my brother Kody."

"Okay, so where do we look for your mom first?" I asked, pushing my plate with the untouched burger and fries on it aside. I scanned the crowd of the small diner we were sitting in to see if anyone was paying attention to us while still listening to Kali.

"Well, I doubt that she's at my grandmother's house because they can only get along for five minutes at a time before they wanna kill each other. The guy that she use to run with, the one she got sentenced to life in prison for, he has a brother named Tony who stays somewhere out here. She'll seek him out because he might be the only person who hasn't turned their back on her."

"I thought my father killed her ex's family before he broke her out of prison?" I asked.

"I don't think he knew about Tony. The only reason I even know about him is because he's a weirdo who tried to fuck me when he found out I was my mother's daughter. Other than that, he's kept a low profile, especially after the shit his punk -ss brother did. I can find him though."

"Do it," I replied without hesitation.

In my mind, my justification was trying to flush Gini out, but deep down, I hadn't liked the look on Kali's face when she'd described this man. A weirdo could mean a lot of things, but the way her body language shifted subconsciously told me she meant it as him being a predator. I'd dealt with those before in my old life, and in my job as a police officer, so I'd know it when I looked in his eyes. I might even fix it for him. As Kali pulled out her phone and went to work, I pulled out mine and linked up with my father to let him know the angle we were chasing. It had taken an intense two-hour conversation in the middle of the night for him and I to come to some type of understanding.

It was hard for him to see me as a grown-ass woman who'd taken on the responsibility of protecting the streets as a police officer, which meant I could handle myself. I'd come to admire and respect his protectiveness, but ever since I'd started doing more running than fighting back, I'd felt like a big part of me was lost, so I needed for him to let ME be ME. That way we could work together, instead of him trying to stretch himself thin and getting killed trying to save everyone. It had shocked the shit out of me that he actually listened to what I'd had to say, but he did, and we came to terms. He didn't even trip about Kali and I getting married because it was a move that was well-played on our parts, and he respected gamesmanship. Our marriage had somewhat of the desired effect too, because he agreed to let us go at Gini while he focused on the real opps that needed killing. It felt good to be seen as my father's daughter and his equal, and for the first time, I knew peace unlike before in my spirit.

"Tony has a house not far from here," Kali said.

I signaled Benji, who was sitting a few tables away from us with four of his men, and he immediately came to our table.

"We're gonna pull up on a dude named Tony and see if our target is there. No one shoots unless fired upon, or unless we start shooting first. Understood?"

"Yes ma'am."

"We'll roll out in five minutes," I said, already texting my father the same information about our plans.

"Where's your dad?" Kali asked.

"Meeting with one of his niggas from back in the day, and then he's gonna decide who to go at first. We're gonna move with coordinated attacks against IG, and the Camaro Cartel," I replied.

"Me and my men will head out now, Mrs. Hawkins, and then I'll signal for you two to come out," Benji said, waving his men into motion as he walked away.

"Have you given any thought to the problem with the police? It seems like their beef is following you, because we don't know if ole boy was impersonating a cop, or if that's really his day job. The hotel asking for discretion right now makes sense, but it leaves us with unanswered questions. It would make sense that crooked cops would stick together, and I'm sure you can find some on any police force, which would explain how we were targeted after we posted about our marriage on social media while in L.A. I think the problem starts down here though, so we need to figure out what cops here in Virginia are after you," Kali said.

"I've been thinking about that too, and the only thing that makes sense is that it’s someone who has a problem with Leroy. That goes back to my sister Cyn's stepfather Steve, which makes the logical place to look is Steve's family, or those loyal enough to pull the trigger for him after he was dead and gone. Whatever is left of those friends and family," I replied.

"Is there anyone who can get you that information from the inside?" Kali asked.

The name that popped up on the tip of my tongue was one I hadn't seen cross my mind in a while because of all the craziness, but now seemed like as good a time as any to find out if he was still in my corner.

"My partner on the police force is a dude that I grew up with named Honcho, and I think I can reach out to him."

"Do it," Kali said.

I complied by sending Honcho a quick text telling him that I was back in town and that I needed to speak with him ASAP. I didn't give him my exact location or any information that could lead someone to me right now, just preferring to play it safe for the moment. By the time I was done sending the first message, Benji was signaling for us to come out.

"Let's move," I said, pulling a $50 dollar bill out of my pocket and leaving it on the table beside my plate.

Ever since I'd made the decision to retake control of my life mentally, my instincts had returned to form, thereby sharpening my senses, so when we stepped out of the diner, I felt confident instead of unbearably anxious. I knew that anybody could be touched, so I wasn't walking around with my chest poked out on some delusional superhero type shit. I was simply comfortable in my own skin again, and I knew that Kali had contributed to that in different ways. Her energy was a forcefield that I drew from often, but I felt like it was vice versa. We both hopped into the back of the waiting 2028 forest-green Ford expedition, and we were whisked away into the night while being followed by a truck identical to ours.

"Here's the location," Kali said, pulling it up on her phone before flinging it to the truck's GPS system.

A few seconds later, the address popped up on the dashboard's screen, accompanied by verbal commands issuing directions to the location. We rode in silence other than the GPS, which made the sounds of my checking and loading my weapon louder in the confines of the dark truck. I had the Ruger P210 .45 strapped to my hip, and the AR-15 was in my lap. Kali was toting a Draco 74 with a hundred-round banana clip, equipped with laser sight and fully automatic selected fire. It was a masterpiece because of its internal cooling system wired throughout the gun's frame to prevent overheating and jamming, and the both of us were eager to witness is awesome power.

It took us ten minutes to pull up in front of Tony's one-story house, which looked pitch black from the inside out. We spent another fifteen minutes watching our surroundings, along with the house, just to let the night settle in around us. Once it became clear that the block was asleep, I nodded for Benji to lead us out of the truck.

"Three men take the back, one man stays put to make sure we're not ambushed or walking into a firefight on our way out, and Benji, you come with us," I instructed, pulling the slide on my gun and flipping the safety off.

I heard a lot of other weapons do the same, which signaled readiness. We approached the house with stealth and speed, and there was no hesitation in my movements as I walked straight up to the front door and booted it open. The police force and academy had prepared me for moments like this, so I was in my element as soon as the sound of wood splintering reached my ears. From there, my instincts took over, allowing me to clear the rooms within seconds while making myself a difficult to hit moving target. By the time Benji's people had breached the back door, I was standing in Tony's bedroom, over top of him and an ugly blonde who was sleeping soundly beside him.

"Wakey-wakey," I said, hitting Tony viciously in the stomach with the butt of my AR-15.

The trifling muthafucka gasped and farted at the same time, but the sight that his eyes popped open to made him lose control of his bowels completely. He shit on himself quicker than a newborn baby.

"Ugh!" Kali said from behind me, stifling an urge to gag.

"I only got ONE question, Tony. Where's Gini?" I asked calmly.

"Who-who the fuck are you, bitch?" the blonde asked.

Kali stepped to her side of the bed, and quickly rendered her unconscious again after several smacks to the head from her Draco.

"Still waiting on that answer Tony," I said, giving him my undivided attention.

"I don't-I don't know any Gini," he replied, cradling his stomach.

"Now's not the time for lies Tony," Kali said, leaning over and putting her gun to his dick.

Suddenly his stomach stopped hurting enough for him to look at Kali and recognize who she was, and that recognition showed all over his pudgy little face.

"Where is she, Tony?" I asked again, already growing tired of repeating myself.

"I don't know. I-I ain't  seen her. Ain't she dead?" he asked, playing dumb even though he really was NOT playing.

"You probably should've led with that last response because THEN your bullshit might've been believable. Now I know you're lying, and that's so disrespectful," I said, handing Benji my AR-15 and pulling my pistol out.

"Wait, I don't—"

That was as far as he got before I took aim at his left kneecap and put a nice round hole in it. His screams were loud, which made them dangerous, but my guess was that nobody would call the cops around here.

"Last time, Tony. Where is Gini?" I asked slowly.

"She's-she's not here, she's gone," he cried, clearly in pain.

"WHERE, Tony?" I asked, placing the warm barrel of my pistol to his exposed and vulnerable right kneecap.

"I don't know, I swear I don't know. He-he picked her up yesterday on his bike and they left!" he yelled.

"WHO picked her up?" Kali asked.

"Dude with a Predator helmet on," he replied rapidly, suddenly a whole lot more cooperative now that he was bleeding.

Kali looked at me, confused, but I had an idea of who we were looking for - or at least which direction to look in.

"Thanks, Tony. Good night," I said sweetly, raising my pistol to his eye level and squeezing off one round.

"Do you know who he was talking about?" Kali asked as we turned and left.

"I think so, but I gotta call my dad."

We made it safely back to the truck and pulled off with no one seemingly the wiser about what had just taken place. I thought that I would've felt guilty over killing a man in cold blood, but I didn't, and maybe that was because nobody connected to this was innocent. Maybe it was the fact that Tony had had that look of a predator. Maybe it was because losing Imani, and then Charlene, had done something to me. I didn't know the answer for sure, and now really wasn't the time to care. I could always go to therapy later. From my point of view, now was the time to up the score with the opps, and that meant anyone on their team could get it. I pulled my phone out and called my dad instead of texting him, and thankfully, he answered on the second ring.

"You okay?" he asked immediately.

"Yeah, we're good, but I need to ask you something. That day you came to my house...when Cyn…when you—"

"I know when you mean, Lia, what about it?" he interjected softly, saving me from saying the words.

"You had a custom bike helmet with you, a predator helmet from the movie, and it matched the bike you had. Was that yours?"

"No. I borrowed it because I'd had to get away from my apartment undetected. That bike and helmet belong to IG, the president over the Nation of Rulers. Why?"

Instantly, it all made sense, and I knew that Tony hadn't wasted his last breath to tell me another lie, but this truth only complicated matters.

"Why, Lia?" he asked again.

"Because Gini was last seen getting on that bike yesterday," I replied.

The phone went silent, but I could hear my dad thinking, and that always felt more lethal than impulse reactions from him. I wondered what a day in the life inside the mind of Leroy Bly was like, and all I could imagine were those old westerns where the town was deserted because death was coming. Death was in the air, and caked into the endless dirt that stretched for miles in every direction. Leroy's mind was THAT kind of dangerous, and I could feel him getting ready to unleash on all who dared stand in his way.

"I want you and Kali to come back to Kentucky ASAP," he said.

"I need to take care of this police issue first, Pops, but as soon as I do, we'll head that way."

"Keep me posted, and call if you need anything else," he replied, disconnecting the call.

"What did he say? Does he know who my mom is with?" Kali asked anxiously.

"Yeah, he knows. It's IG," I replied, looking over at her.

Even in the shadows of the SUV, I could see the fear on her face, and I knew where it was coming from. We were trying to save her mom, but her mom kept digging a deeper grave for herself. We both knew that we were running out of time.

"What are we gonna do, babe?" Kali asked, sounding utterly defeated in the moment.

"We stick to the plan. We keep this family TOGETHER by any means necessary, or we die trying."

# CHAPTER 12

*Leroy*

*Alexandria, Virginia*

"Frank! Ayo, FRANK!" I hollered, banging on his apartment door again for the seventh time straight.

I could hear movement coming from the other side of the door, and his baby mama had told me which apartment I could find the nigga in, so I didn't understand why he wasn't answering. I knocked one last time and I was about to leave when I heard locks clicking and moving. A few seconds later, I was standing toe to toe with my main man from childhood.

"Damn, Frank, what the fuck took you so long?"

"Why the fuck is your bama ass out here banging on my shit like the federales?"

"What's wrong, my nigga, you nervous?" I taunted, grinning like I'd just discovered a secret.

"Nervous? Me, get nervous? Slim, do you know where you at? You standing in 2408 Fairhaven, at the top of Huntington, on THE Richmond Highway, slim. This ain't Alexandria, and I ain't none of them farmers you know who gets shaky. My name is NOODLES, nigga, and you can take that up and down the highway like a black Amex card, because it's good everywhere."

I kept a straight face for as along as I could, and then I grabbed two handfuls of his shiny big black beard and pulled on it playfully.

"Let go of my damn face, slim," he said, laughing and slapping my hands away before trying to hit me.

I laughed with him as I dapped him up, and he pulled me inside his apartment. Me and Noodles went back a long way and had been in the trenches where real niggas was few and far between. We'd stuck together, never folded, and had remained solid throughout life, but I only called on him when I really needed to because I respected that he lived a different life now. This was one of those moments, but the moment I stepped inside the apartment, the smells of sweat and blood filled my nose, causing me to look at my man closer. Noodles stood 6'3", 220 pounds, with his brown-skinned bald head protected by his black kufi in representation of his being a Sunni Muslim. There was always the light of humor in his brown eyes, unless there was an issue, because THEN you got to see the difference between Frank and Noodles. From the look on his face, the disheveled look of his clothing, and the smells that had caught my attention coming in, I'd say that Noodles was in rare form.

"Am I interrupting something, bruh?" I asked seriously, glancing around the apartment casually, yet closely.

"Nah, not really. You know it's different when you own a building and you try to handle the repairs yourself instead of outsourcing them to contractors."

"Well, who told you to buy the building, or the entire apartment complex, for that matter? Most niggas who made the type of money you did in the dope game bought themselves houses and land far removed from the pissy apartments they grew up in, but not you. You wanted to save this place, like it's a shrine, so don't complain now," I stated.

"You're right about most of what you said, but I didn't buy this neighborhood to make it a shrine. I bought it to save some kid like it saved me when my mother moved us down here from New Jersey. I bought this apartment complex because it'll always be home, no matter where I'm at in the world, and I takes care of home," he replied passionately.

I'd known this man long enough to know just how good his intentions were, so I wasn't about to disrespect him by questioning him now. Something more was at play though, and I needed to get past that so that I had his undivided attention.

"Listen, my nigga, I got a situation that's moving fast, and I need you, but first I need you to let me help you. What's really good?" I asked.

He looked at me for a long moment before motioning for me to follow him further into the apartment. He led me to a back bedroom, and when he opened the door, the smell of sweat and blood came booming out like nerve gas, causing my stomach to roll. I spotted the source of the odors as a badly beaten light-skinned man and a white woman lying prone on the floor, barely conscious. The face of the man was almost impossible to recognize, yet it seemed familiar. I knew who the white girl was because she was a hoe that had been in the game for years. Victoria was a blonde-haired, blue-eyed, ugly Barbie type that had been passed around Northern Virginia until her pussy was stretched out like I-495. I'd met her in Annandale when we were both just teenagers, and she'd had fun with me and the homies, but a hoe wasn't built to be a housewife. The last I'd heard was that she'd gone to work for the state of Virginia in some capacity, trying to clean up her image as a whore and heroin addict so that she could land herself a respectable husband. If the dude laying next to her was supposed to be that, then everybody had lost.

"What's this, bruh?" I asked.

"This is a little situation that the brothers asked me to handle. You might remember this nigga from when we did that short bid together out at Nottoway. Fake pretty boy type, cold rat, supposedly from Mississippi with his country ass."

"Justice," I replied, vaguely remembering who he was describing as his face came into focus in my mind.

"Yeah, that's the bama nigga. He's been walking around saying that he's Muslim like he represents Sunni, but in real life, he practices Moorish Science."

"Okay, well I know it's no joke to play with religion, but is that all that led to this?" I asked, gesturing towards the obvious results of a dedicated ass whooping.

In response to my question, Noodles pulled out his phone and began searching for something. Once he found it, he handed me the phone, and I saw a video waiting to be played. I hit the button not knowing what was coming, but as soon as the action started, I understood what had led to the vicious ass whooping. I was damn near tempted to put boots to this trifling-ass nigga myself in the name of Allah. The video showed Justice naked on all fours, with a man's dick deep down his throat playing tag with his Adam's apple, while Victoria fucked him in the ass with a big black strap-on dildo. Based on the technique and rhythm, it was clear that this wasn't their first rodeo, which made me laugh and gag at the same time.

"I know you all was KILLING IT on Only Fans! That is NOT how you pray," I said, shaking my head in disgust.

"That ain't even funny, slim, and that's why these muthafuckas had to get touched. I don't expect shit from this smut-ass bitch because she's been a hoe, but for this nigga to be claiming Islamic beliefs and doing this is unacceptable."

"I get it. So kill them and let's get down to business," I said simply.

"I can't do that because the Imam hasn't sanctioned that yet."

I thought about the rock and hard place this put my man in because on the one hand, he knew the right thing to do, but on the other hand, he had to follow protocol. Not to mention the danger of keeping them alive like this because anything could happen to bring attention to this shit. It needed to be handled sooner rather than later, period.

"Is the nigga Justice Sunni Muslim or not?" I asked.

"No, he ain't with us."

That simplified things in my mind, so I pulled out my pistol and shot both of them three times in the head. Noodles looked at the bodies, and then looked back at me.

"I like that gun, slim. Is it new?" he asked.

"Yeah, and I'll tell you all about it later, but now we need to discuss the business."

He nodded while leading me from the room, and closing the door behind us. We went to the kitchen, where he pulled out a bottle of Hennessey and a couple glasses, and we sat down at the kitchen table. After we tossed back a couple shots apiece, we got down to the details.

"So what's up, slim, what brings you back to the highway all of a sudden?" he asked.

"How much do you want to know?"

"Only as much as I need to. You know I'm not a nosy type nigga," he replied.

"Well then, the important part that I need from you is info on Zuk's baby mama Jennifer and their kids. I need to know any place that he would consider safe to lay his head."

"You say Zuk? I thought that was you mans, slim? I mean I ain't tripping, but you know that information costs around these parts. Just consider it a toll road fee for access to the beltway," he said, smiling.

"Not an issue. Just give me the price and the place where you want the money transferred to," I said, pulling out my phone.

When he held his hand out, I passed him my phone, and when he was done, he gave it back. $100k seemed like a fair price considering that this was a rush job and I didn't know whose palms he had to grease, so I sent it to the account number he'd provided.

"It'll be available in 30 minutes," I said.

"I should have what you need by then, and I'll shoot it to your phone."

"Good looking, my nigga. I'll be in touch sooner rather than later, and we can hit up Gums Springs to shoot some ball or something," I said.

“Tighten up, slim. You know you can't fuck with me inside them four lines, so just stay on the sideline where it’s safe. Remember to stay sucka free too. I don't know what's going on, but if you're seeking to destroy the niggas closest to you, then you probably picked the wrong niggas to get close to. That's just food for thought, brother to brother."

"And I appreciate that," I replied sincerely, dapping him up.

I left the apartment intending to jump back on the task I front of me, but a text to my phone had me pause on my bike in the parking lot. The first thing that came through was a text from Erin with the info from her private investigator about the Camaro Cartel's operations in Virginia, and I immediately forwarded that to Phantom with instructions to dismantle shit. Before I could pull off though, Erin texted me again, telling me that Matt wanted to see me now, and giving me his location. I saw the address, recognized it immediately, and chuckled softly because it was familiar from our old days. I knew that there was no avoiding him forever, so I might as well get it over with. I texted her back and told her to let him know that I was on the way, and then I pointed my bike in the direction of D.C.

It took me half an hour to reach the Bloody Knuckles boxing gym on the southeast side of the city, and I came in through the back door. Of course Matt was already there, sitting on the side of the main ring with two sets of 10-ounce gloves next to him. There wasn't another soul in the gym, and I could tell the instant that Matt heard me enter because he stood up and pulled his shirt off.

Standing 6’4” with sandy blonde hair, weighing 215 pounds, the military had made sure that he'd kept his body in fine tune and it was easy for me to see. The look in his eyes wasn't exactly murderous, but it damn sure wasn't friendly either. Right before I reached the ring, my phone vibrated with two different texts. The first one was the info I'd paid Noodles for, which I quickly forwarded to Phantom with instructions for his men to round up everybody and wait for further instructions. The second text was from Erin, and it was a picture of her naked blowing me a kiss with the words GOOD LUCK attached. I chuckled softly, sent her a reply, and then turned my attention to the mountain in front of me that needed climbing.

"Matthew."

"Leroy," he replied in the same neutral tone.

I pulled my shirt off while putting my gun down, and then we laced our gloves up before climbing in the ring.

"Nothing personal," I said, holding my hands out.

He chuckled, but it didn't escape me that there was no humor in it at all.

"It's ALL personal, Leroy, so bring your best."

Before I could utter another word, he fired a straight stiff jab that hit the sweet spot between my nose and mouth, snapping my head back with a bullet's impact. I tasted blood instantly, and my eyes watered, but I could feel myself smiling. This was gonna be fun.

# CHAPTER 13

*Lia*

"Damn, I didn't think I'd see your ass again," Honcho said, scooping me up in a huge hug as soon as he got out of his truck.

I'd been hesitant to meet up with him in person, but Kali given me a pep talk which included luring him into territory that gave us all the advantages. If he refused or showed fear, then that was a clear sign that his alliance was in question at the least, and he was suspect at best. I knew the property where Charlene had kept me safe wasn't far away, and when I'd reached out to my dad, he'd given me the exact address. I'd passed it on to Honcho, and the rest was history, because here he stood.

"With everything going on, I just had to get away for a while, you know? I'm sorry I didn't reach out before now," I said.

"You don't owe me any apologies, Lia, I get it. At first, I thought that- you know, the situation at your condo - I thought that was you. We all did. Then the autopsy revealed that it was Imani, but we still didn't know where you were. Rumors began to fly in the department, but you know I don't pay attention to that shit. I'm a cop first, so I relied on that, and I eventually tracked down Brisha. Once she told me that you were okay and headed out of town, I was able to breathe easier, and I figured that you'd reach out eventually. You had plenty of vacation time built up, so I just squared it with the boss."

"How did they take that?" I asked nonchalantly.

"At first they were pissed about not knowing where you were, and they kept questioning me about your whereabouts like I was some kind of perp or something. I couldn't tell them what I didn't know, and I wouldn't have told them anyway because you deserved to grieve in solitude. I'm glad you took that time though, because you look good," he said, smiling down at me as he held me at arm's length.

Even though there was absolutely nothing sexual in the look, or in the energy between Honcho and me, I could feel Kali's eye's watching us intensely from over my shoulder.

"I'd like to think that I've had a hand in the glow she's sporting," Kali said, stepping forward.

"I bet you have, and congratulations to both of you. I'm Honcho," he replied, letting me go and holding his hand out to her.

She took it and shook it, but not before putting space between him and me, which made me smile inwardly.

"Come on, let's catch up. I got us a bottle and some good gas," he said, patting the pockets of his jacket.

"This way," I replied, leading the way into the house and into the kitchen, where we could all pull up seats at the table.

"So, Lia tells me that she saved your ass when you two were younger. Is that true?" Kali asked innocently.

I laughed from reflex at the memory of his hours spent in jail fighting for his virginity, but I saw the embarrassment heat up his face before he was able to suppress it and laugh it off.

"We both saved each other, and we've got stories to tell, but some shit remains a kept secret between us," he replied, giving me a pointed look.

"There's nothing to be ashamed of, Honcho. She saved my life too," Kali said, smiling at me.

"Likewise, babe," I said, smiling at her over my shoulder as I grabbed glasses for all of us. By the time I got to the kitchen table, Kali and Honcho both had sat down and managed to strategically position me in the middle, which I thought was cute.

"So Honcho, what types of shit was you hearing while I was gone?" I asked.

"Nothing worth repeating, trust me."

"Yeah, but probably entertaining nonetheless, especially if Commander Montgomery had her dick-sucking lips involved," I persisted, playing a hunch while pouring drinks from the bottle he'd slid me.

"I mean, there was talk about you disappearing with your pops, because nobody knew for sure where that nigga ghosted to neither," he said, carefully rolling a blunt.

My eyes slid in Kali's direction, and I communicated in silence to let her know that there was a problem with his statement. I couldn't elaborate without being suspicious, but I knew that she'd take the look I gave her and be on point.

"Why the fuck would they be their first thought?" I asked, feigning confusion and glossing over the fact that Honcho shouldn't know that Leroy was my father. It was possible that he saw the same thing on the news feed that Imani had on the day she died, but I needed to be sure, so I kept pushing.

"I mean, I guess that they didn't buy the coincidence of you playing dead the day your spot blew up at the same time your pops was released and went underground. You already know that as cops, we're taught to be suspicious before practical, so coincidence is like the unicorn's existence, " he said.

"Ain't that the truth," I said, pushing him his cup and looking at Kali.

I watched out the corner of my eye as one of her hands reached for the glass I'd slid her way, while the other hand slid under the table to the gun in her waist.

"How many people know that I was playing dead?" I asked offhandedly.

"Just the ones..." His voice trailed off as his hands suddenly became increasingly preoccupied with the blunt in his hands, but the way his eyes locked on my face told his secret.

"How would the cops, your coworkers, know that she wasn't dead unless they were there and saw her escape?" Kali asked calmly before tossing her shot back and setting her glass gently back on the table.

"I-I don't know how they knew. I think it was-it was just a hunch, because Lia is such a good cop," he replied shakily.

"Come on, Honcho, you can do better than that, bruh," I said, feeling the disappointment spread throughout my chest with the speed of the potent liquor I'd tossed down my throat.

"Wh-what do you mean, shawty? I told you what I think, and that's all I know," he replied somewhat defiantly as he lit the blunt.

I let him fill his lungs with a few hits of the potent-smelling loud pack without saying a word, but I could tell by how he fidgeted that he was feeling the weight of the silence.

"So, uh, how long are you gonna be in Richmond?" he asked, making a lame play for small talk.

This time when I looked at Kali, I gave her a nod, which caused her to pull her Sig Sauer P365 xmacro 9mm pistol and place it on the tabletop in front of her. Honcho's eyes immediately went to the pistol, and by the time he looked at me I was holding a two-tone Taurus G3c 9mm pistol casually in my grip on the table.

"We go back a long way, bruh, and for that reason I don't wanna have to torture you. Don't test me though," I warned, looking him directly in the eyes.

"Nod if you understand," Kali demanded.

Once he did that, I motioned for him to continue smoking the weed. He hesitated long enough to look at me and Kali again, and then he hit it lightly. The smell if marijuana was definitely strong, but it didn't completely mask the smell of whatever it was laced with.

"Who knows you're here?" I asked.

"C-Commander Montgomery, and her fiancé, Sergeant Conyers."

"Who is Sergeant Conyers?" I asked, confused by the new name and player in the game.

"He's not from our district originally, but he's been around ever since you went missing. All I know is that his dad and your dad have history, and not in a good way."

Kali and I exchanged a look because it seemed like we'd found the needle in the haystack of cops with an axe to grind against Leroy, and his family by extension.

"What did they tell you to do?" I asked.

"Just to make sure you smoked the blunt down to the end and drank all the liquor, then text them. They would handle it from there."

"Okay, so text them," Kali instructed.

He gladly dropped the blunt in the ashtray and slowly pulled his phone out of his pocket. "What now?" he asked after sending the message that his mission was a success.

"We wait," I replied, gesturing with my gun for him to pick the blunt back up and resume smoking.

With reluctance, he followed my directive, and I didn't feel the slightest bit of compassion for the pleading look in his eyes. Within a few minutes his phone pinged, and Kali motioned for him to slide it across the table to her. Once she read the text message, she slid the phone to me and pulled out her own phone. The reply message was short and left nothing to the imagination because it simply read, “make your excuses to leave because we're sending shooters.” I chuckled, and then I slid the phone back to him. He read the message, and his eyes immediately swung to mine.

"Can-can I leave? I promise—"

"You promise nothing, but to die," Kali said, raising her gun and firing two shots into his face.

The force from the bullet's impact tossed his entire body up and over the back of the chair, but a mixture of blood and brain fragments remained on the tabletop. For some reason, my eyes stayed glued to that, and I could feel the tears stinging my eyes, but I refused to let them fall. The nigga had brought it on himself, and I owed it to Imani to see all those who played a part in plotting against me get what was coming to them. I would've slumped the bitch-ass nigga myself, but I was grateful to Kali for doing it for me. When I finally looked in her direction, I saw the sympathy she felt for me, and that pushed me out of the chair so that I could step into her arms. She held me tightly for a moment, and that was all I needed to center myself.

"Did you alert Benji to our guests' arrival?" I asked, taking a tiny step back.

"Yeah, and they're ready. We need to move his truck and get ready."

I nodded my understanding, but I couldn't bring myself to go near Honcho's body. Thankfully, Kali sensed this because she moved over to him, and a few moments later, she was back, pressing his keys into my palm.

"You move his truck, and I'll do the rest," she said, kissing me on the forehead.

I nodded and walked back towards the front of the house where he'd parked. I blocked off the images that tried to flood my mind as I climbed behind the wheel of his 2026 smoke grey GMC Denali and focused on the fight that was coming. After I hid the truck, I ran back into the house and went straight to the gun safe Charlene had shown me what seemed like a lifetime ago. Remaining focused on what was coming this whole time had kept me distracted from the pain of Charlene's memory being everywhere in this house. I hadn't realized how being back here would've affected me, and at first, I didn't notice it, but Kali did. She saw my hands shaking when we first arrived and were coming into the house, so she'd grabbed my hand and given me her energy as a security blanket. I felt the need for it again arise right now as I stood looking at the arsenal inside the gun safe, but I was able to push through. I grabbed and loaded the grenade launcher before slipping the strap with the AK-47 attached to it over my head so that the assault rifle was resting comfortably against my chest. After stuffing an extra clip in my pocket, I closed the safe and made my way back to the kitchen to meet up with Kali. Thankfully, Honcho's body was gone, so I didn't have to face that again. At some point, I'd grieve the loss of that relationship, because burying that kind of pain could destroy me in the end, but now wasn't the time for that.

"You ready?" Kali asked, coming up behind me.

"Yeah, let's do this."

Kali led the way outside into the darkness, but she looked to me to lead us to the best vantage spot for our attack. Benji and his team were posted about half a mile up the road to make sure there were no survivors trying to escape. The goal wasn't to keep them out, because we wanted everyone to step into the trap before it slammed shut. We made it to the edge of the clearing of the driveway, and by then, I could hear the sounds of car engines in the distance.

"Over here," I said, ducking behind some wildly growing hedges.

We set up in a way that allowed us to open fire at every vehicle whether they were ahead of us in the driveway roundabout or still coming up the driveway. After what seemed like an eternity, the sounds of engines came close enough for me to make out the silhouette of two slow-moving cars. I couldn't see how many occupants were inside each vehicle, so I chose to err on the side of caution and go BIG first. As soon as the cars came to a stop, I popped up out of the bushes with the grenade launcher in my hands, and I shot a grenade into each car's window. Whoever was inside only had time to open a car door before both vehicles exploded, sending eight tires into the air like the car was playing hopscotch. I dropped the grenade launcher at my feet and readied the AK-47 just in case there were survivors. After a couple of minutes of nothing but bright flames and the smell of hot flesh permeating the air, I texted Benji to tell him that we were coming out.

"What's next?" Kali asked once we were in our truck with me behind the wheel.

"I doubt the commander or the sergeant were in either of those cars, so now we pay them a visit," I replied.

"Ohhh, I LOVE making house calls!"

# CHAPTER 14

*Leroy*

"Your technique was crisper when you'd just got out of prison. You started getting money and you got soft," he said.

"Yeah? Well, I can tell that your military career has almost reached the retirement phase because you move slower than you ever have," I replied.

"You wanna go again so I can teach you how to salute an officer properly?"

"Only if you wanna taste more of your own blood, and see more stars than the flag you represent can hold," I replied, smiling at him.

We'd been sitting on the side of the ring, talking shit to each other since both of our knees had given out thirty minutes ago. Just like so many of our fights back in the day, there was no clear-cut winner, but the goal of this game had always been about respect. Matt was the type who felt ENTITLED to respect, and I was the type to believe you had to EARN it, so we'd fought a lot in our younger years.

"I swear that the next time we step into that ring, I'ma break something on you," he vowed.

I laughed out loud even though I knew how serious he was because this was basically his way of saying this was over for the moment. I was glad, because my endurance was NOT up there with his right now. He got paid to stay in shape, and it was money well spent as far as I was concerned.

"Look, L, I love you like a brother, but Erin IS family, and she's my favorite sister. You KNEW better," he said, shaking his head disapprovingly.

"It's more complicated then what I KNEW, bruh, but I give you my word that I'll stand beside her or in front of her for the rest of time. I just finished putting Daniel in his place before coming out here to play your punching bag."

"Oh yeah? I bet that felt good," he said, smiling genuinely for the first time.

"If it was up to me I would've just killed him and fixed the problem permanently, but I'm trying to be a better person and let your nephews keep their father. If he keeps fucking with Erin though, I'ma put half a dozen holes and dents in his skull just to give his brains someplace to breathe through."

"In the meantime though, you have to focus on everything else that's trying to tear you down. Are you making any progress on that?" he asked, pulling his gloves off.

"Yeah, but I'm moving strategically to preserve and maintain the element of surprise. I've called in some favors, made a couple of useful allies for the short and long haul, and now I'm in a position to strike from multiple angles simultaneously," I replied, taking my own gloves off and stretching to avoid body tightness.

"I've got a transport coming in with more guns and bullets for you, and all I need is a location to ship them to once they land in Virginia."

"Not a problem. But I've got a bigger favor to ask of you," I said, looking at him squarely in the eye. "If this shit goes sideways, and not in my favor, I need you to make sure my daughter Lia is good. I know I don't have to ask you anything when it comes to the baby your sister is carrying, but I need that same treatment and energy for my oldest daughter as well."

"You know I'll make sure Lia is good, along with everyone else you love. Try not to let it come to that though because you're still my brother for life, and I'm in the mood to hunt down muthafuckas."

"And you're my brother too. No worries; I'm good," I replied genuinely, reaching my hand out to him.

He took it and pulled me into a clumsy hug before trying to slip me into a headlock. We both laughed as we grappled, but eventually, the knee pain made us sit our asses down again.

"Come on, you can bring me up to speed while we go get something to eat," he said.

"Sounds like a plan."

I pulled my shirt back on and put everything back in my pockets before tucking my gun in the waist of my jeans. When I checked my phone, I saw that I'd missed two calls, and I had text messages from Phantom that put a smile on my face. During my half hour sparring session, Phantom had mobilized his troops, and he told me to expect results within the hour. I replied to his text and sent a few of my own before following Matt outside to the parking lot.

"New bike?" he asked.

"Yeah, just one of the favors I had to call in," I replied nonchalantly.

"I'd say that's a hell of a favor considering how rare this Ducati is, but I admire your taste. Keep me in mind if you wanna get rid of it," he said, smiling mischievously.

We both knew that this was his not-so-subtle way of telling me he wanted my bike, without him coming right out and saying I owed it to him. All I could do was smile back as I climbed on the beast and grabbed my helmet.

"Where are we going?" I asked.

"One of your restaurants. It's been a long time since I had some of your mother's southern cooking, and I know all you use are her and Candice's recipes."

"We can fix that. Just follow me. Keep up though, because this bitch is FAST," I said, starting the bike and pulling off with my front tire facing the sky in a wild wheelie.

It only took us fifteen minutes to pull up at one of my spots on M Street, and we crept in through the back kitchen entrance.

"Bring me two of the day's specials to my private table in the back corner of the restaurant's main floor," I instructed April, a waitress I spotted.

"Right away, Mr. Bly."

I could tell that everyone was surprised to see me because it had been so long since I'd come through, which wasn't how I'd done business since any of my restaurants had opened. I liked to be hands on, but life was very different from the days when I'd make my rounds checking on the empire, and a part of me missed those simpler times. The way my life was set up now called for me to leave the micromanaging to the people I paid to handle those things. My eyes were scanning everything and taking it all in as I led Matt to our table, and I didn't see anything to complain about, which made me proud as a business owner. It wasn't too crowded because the lunch rush was over, but by dinner time, this bitch would be booming again.

"You want something to drink, bruh?" I asked.

"Sweet tea is always good here."

I made sure to pass our drink orders on to another waiter as we neared my private table, and as soon as I did, my eye caught something that changed my mental focus. I didn't let it outwardly show that I was suddenly on high alert, but my instincts were humming away at high speed. When we sat down, I made sure that my back was to the wall and Matt was at an angle that was easy to take cover from as my eyes scanned the entire restaurant.

"What's up?" Matt asked suddenly.

"What do you mean?"

"I mean that I know you, and right now your ears are pinned back like a dog either looking to fight or hunt. In your case, it could be both, so what's up?" he asked again, casually scanning the restaurant under the ruse of a new diner.

"It's not unusual for Nation of Rulers members to eat at my establishments, but when I came in, I spotted three different Rulers dressed in regular clothes without their leathers, not eating. And now there are only two of them visible, which leads me to believe that the other went to make a call."

"Okay, so how do you wanna play this?" he asked calmly.

"I'm sure you've got a gun on you, and this ain't nothing we can't handle, but I don't know what's coming, and we could find ourselves outgunned and outnumbered."

"Not in my city," he replied simply, casually slipping his phone out and working his fingers faster than a concert pianist.

Meanwhile, I was doing my best to continue observing the restaurant and gauging the temperature of my fellow club members. They were trying not to stand out, but the fact that they were just flagging down the waiter to order food didn't come off casual or smooth. When I first peeped them, it had already looked like they had been here for a while. They'd been on a mission of observation, so the question was, who sent them? I was hesitant to pull out my phone just because I could feel their eyes on me, but the waiter arriving with our drink order created the perfect distraction in the moment. With my phone in my hand, I quickly analyzed who could offer some support swiftly should the need arise.

"We've got help inbound, ETA seven minutes," Matt said without glancing up from his phone.

By process of logical elimination, I knew that only IG or Zuk would've made the call to have Rulers watching my spots, so I decided to poke a bear. I sent both men an invitation through text to join me for a late lunch at my current location. Part of me was kicking myself because I'd insisted that the security Erin had hired focus on her and Lia, which was why I was running these streets solo like The Flash. It was hella arrogant of me, and it might cost me in the end.

"Good afternoon, Mr. Bly. Here are our infamous complementary buttermilk biscuits that come with every order," April said, setting the basket down next to my glass of sweet tea.

"Thank you," I replied absentmindedly, resuming my observation of the restaurant.

"You good, bruh? How do you wanna handle this?" Matt asked once the waiter was gone.

"I'd prefer for it not to get ugly with this many witnesses, because that will only lead to having to explain it officially when the blood starts flowing. At the time, you and I are gonna walk out of here the same way we walked in this bitch. Regardless of who gotta die," I stated, looking at him knowingly.

He nodded thoughtfully, but there wasn't an ounce of fear in his eyes or demeanor. "I'm gonna make a quick run to the truck, and you just keep your head on a swivel, soldier," he said, sliding out of his seat and heading for the kitchen.

I nodded, but inwardly, I was battling my desire to feel my gun in my grip to comfort me. Instead, all I had was my phone, which was providing me with absolutely no calm or reassurance should this shit turn on a dime and go bad quickly.

No sooner had that thought crossed my mind then the front door to the restaurant opened and in walked Zuk, followed by three more Rulers. Quick math told me that the odds were now 7-2, not in our favor, and I was currently all alone with the potential opps. I played it cool, choosing to remain seated and let them come to me, because I was banking on the fact that nobody wanted to get too active in public - especially when we were so close to the Navy Yard. I watched Zuk scan the room until his eyes locked on me, and then he and his helpers made a beeline for my table. With Matt not being here, it kind of gave us an advantage because we now had the element of surprise, which could fuck with the numbers advantage they had. Right now, stalling was my best option, and I always played the hand I was dealt.

"'Sup Zuk? I know you want some of this good food, don't you?" I asked, smiling widely.

"Nah, I'm not really hungry," he replied, taking a seat across from me without waiting for the invitation.

The Rulers flanking him wore prospect patches, and they weren't faces that I recognized, but I ignored them completely as they stood behind Zuk like lost puppies.

"Well, if you didn't come for the food, then what brings you by, my brother?" I asked calmly.

"I think you know why I'm here, L, but if you need me to spell it out for you, I'll keep it simple. IG wants to see you, and that's not up for debate," Zuk replied.

"Damn, you IG's errand boy now, my nigga? Say it ain't so," I said, smiling maliciously.

He didn't give a verbal response, but he didn't have to because the anger clouding his eyes was unmistakable to the trained observer. When my phone pinged in my hands, it broke the staring contest him and I were locked into as I looked down to see who was texting me. What I saw caused a shit-eating grin to spread the width of my face, and I made sure to look up so that Zuk could see every inch of it.

"I think you got bigger things to worry about than making sure IG gets what he wants. Focus on yourself for once, and stop being a "yes man" all your life. I'll go see him when I get ready," I said smugly.

"It don't work like that, Leroy. When the Prez calls, you come. Don't make us cause a scene in here," he replied forcefully.

His words made the young wolves behind him get a little antsy with their movements, but nobody reached for a weapon. I held my phone up purposefully so that Zuk could see it, and then I slowly turned it so that he had a good look at the screen. The distress of seeing his baby mama hogtied was easy to read on his face, but the moment he spotted his kids in the background of the screenshot, watching TV, his whole face crumbled into that of a man on the verge of breaking.

"This shit is chess, not checkers, so you better ALWAYS stay at least a few moves ahead. Or pay the consequences for playing pussy. So, Zuk, who's getting fucked?"

# Chapter 15

*Lia*

"Can you explain to me how a cop lives HERE? I thought you all were paid pennies to serve and protect," Kali said, admiring Commander Montgomery's three-story house that sat alone at the end of a cul-de-sac.

"We're not paid pennies, but we damn sure ain't rolling like THIS. Even as a commander, she would clear maybe 60k after taxes each year, so unless she inherited this spot, I'd say she has another revenue stream," I replied.

There were other houses on the street leading to the house we were now watching, but Commander Montgomery's was the nicest. It wasn't worth it to me to ask the bitch who her realtor was though because all I had on my mind was murder. Cold-blooded murder.

"How do you wanna do this? There are lights shining on two out of the three floors, so we know they're in there. Do you wanna kick the door down on them?" Kali asked.

I kept my eyes focused on the house, but my mind was travelling back into time, and I could feel my body temperature dropping. The part of me that knew I was on the verge of crossing into the darkness was screaming, but the part of me craving the solitude in that dark knew how to quiet those screams. Maybe one day I would regret all the decisions I'd made on this night, but today wasn't that day and this night wasn't over. This moment was mine to embrace.

"I want to do to them EXACTLY what they did to me. Bring 'em out by blasting them out," I replied, texting Benji my plan.

Thirty seconds later, I saw the doors to the truck parked behind us open silently, and then Benji and his team slid out to merge seamlessly with the night around us. I watched as they entered the uncleared wooded area that started where we'd stopped our trucks and wrapped around the back of

Commander Montgomery's property until it ended parallel to us on the opposite side of the street. Kali and I sat in comfortable silence, waiting, and two minutes later, my phone buzzed with the message that let me know Benji was in place.

"Let's go," I said, climbing out of the truck.

Kali was equipped with her Draco and I still had my AK-47 around my chest with the grenade launcher in my hands. Sticking to the densest shadows, I led us to the house, and once we got there, I texted Benji so that he would know what to do next.

"Babe, count to 30 for me," I requested as I checked to see how many grenades I had left.

By the light of the moon, I saw that four of the barrels were loaded, but truthfully, I would've been happy with three. One for each story of the house. Benji knew to hold the back of the property down in case they fled that way, but my goal was to bring them out the front door and right into my arms.

"30," Kali said softly.

"Stay here. I'll be right back," I said, taking off at a slow jog around the side of the house.

When I got there, I quickly picked out my target windows, and then I fired two grenades a piece into the second and third floor windows. Dropping the empty grenade launcher, I took off at a dead run back to where Kali was waiting around the corner. As soon as she saw me, she raised her gun, looking to shoot anyone behind me, but I knew that what was behind me was bigger than bullets. Fire was a living, breathing thing, and I made it just past the corner if the house when I heard the first two fire-starting grenades go off. I was able to stay on my feet and keep moving forward, but when the other two grenades detonated, I was pushed airborne by the blast's force. I was only thrown a few feet across the yard, and it knocked the wind out of me a little bit, but I recovered just as Kali reached me.

"You good?" she asked, pulling me to my feet while keeping her eyes on the now-glowing house behind me.

"Yeah, n-no sweat," I replied, spinning around with my AK-47 at the ready.

Within seconds, the front door opened, and two people came bolting out into the night.

"Leg shots," I said, aiming lower so as to wound first.

Kali did the same, and our weapons sang a sweet duet that left our targets screaming into the night. I knew that we didn't have much time, which meant that I couldn't savor this victory like I wanted to in the moment, but that was okay. Dead was dead, no matter when you celebrated it.

"Text Benji and tell him to get back to the truck," I said, walking over to the couple who were still screaming in agony.

Their neighbors were close enough to have heard the explosion, and they would undoubtedly be able to see the growing flames licking the night sky, which would lead them to come outside. Even with this knowledge relaying through my mind, I still took my time walking over to them. I was taking pleasure in their pain, and the sight of them rolling around on the ground was entertaining as hell. My mind was clouded with the sound of Imani's voice merging with the sounds of her final screams as she lay trapped, and dying, because of the people in front of me. I stood over top of both of them for a few seconds, not fully feeling the satisfaction I desired until I saw the recognition in Montgomery's eyes.

"You should've killed me yourself, bitch. Leroy Bly sends his regards," I said, raising the assault rifle and caressing the trigger with a gentle pull.

I sprayed both of them, feeling a new kind of joy as their bodies twitched wildly from the .223 rounds making them do that dance. I spent half a clip between the two of them, and then I walked away without a backwards glance. The look on Kali's face was one of concern, but she said nothing as we took off running back to our truck. We arrived at the same time Benji and his people emerged from the woods, so everyone was loaded up and moving out within minutes. I watched the steadily growing fire in the rearview mirror, and I could feel the smile taking over my face as feelings beyond my ability to describe took over my spirit. The fight wasn't over, but I'd avenged Imani's murder and kept us safe, which finally put me on the road to forgiving myself for all the things that I couldn't control.

"Are you okay?" Kali asked.

"I don't know... But I know I will be. How 'bout you?"

"Oh yeah, I'm great. This was just another slow Tuesday night for me," she replied sarcastically.

The look on her face when I glanced over at her made me chuckle until full-bellied laughter was echoing throughout the truck from both of us. If anyone who knew what we'd just done could see and hear us now, they'd think that we lost our muthafuckin' minds, or left them back there at the crime scene. I couldn't have said why we were laughing so damn hard, but I knew it felt good to do it.

"Okay, where are we going?" she asked, once we were under control.

"I don't know. I guess we can turn our attention back to finding your mom now and saving her from herself."

"I don't know where to begin that search at this point because I have no idea who IG really is or where he'd go," she replied.

"Shit, I don't either. We can call my dad, but I know he's just gonna tell us to come back to Kentucky."

"Well, then I guess that's our only move right now. Are you good to drive, or do you need me to take over?" she asked, concerned.

"Nah, I'm good. I'm still full of adrenaline from the fireworks display I put on. Can you text Benji and let him know where we're going?"

She pulled her phone out and took care of that while I aimed us at the highway that would take us out of town. For the first time, I was asking myself what I would do once all of this madness was really and truly behind us. One thing I knew for sure was that I'd never be the same young woman I'd been. Kali and I had discussed our business aspirations and goals, but truthfully, there was enough money within our reach to prevent us from having to work if we didn't want to. The real question was, what would life look like for us as squares?

"Can I ask you something, Kali?"

"Sure babe, what's up?"

"Do you want kids?" I asked.

In my peripheral vision, I saw her fingers stop moving on her phone's screen, and I could feel the heat of her staring at me.

"Where did that question come from?"

"I don't know. I'm just trying to imagine what our life is gonna be like when shit calms down and we're taking it day by day. Everything has kinda just been HAPPENING, so there's really never been a moment where we could have this conversation. I'm curious to know what you see for our future, besides business stuff," I said, glancing over at her.

"Kids? Well, yeah, I do want kids actually. I always saw myself as having at least two because I want a boy and a girl. While we're on the subject though, I've been meaning to ask what role dick plays in this relationship?"

"What do you mean?" I asked, slightly confused.

"I mean I'm not gay; I'm bisexual. I LOVE what you can do to my body, and it was definitely an experience worth the wait, but I LOVE me some dick too. Just being honest. And my preference is black men."

"Oh…well I'd never thought about that part. Are you worried that I won't satisfy you all the time? Because—"

"No, baby, it's not that because I KNOW you can satisfy me at all times. Its just...I don't know how to explain it. There's nothing like the feeling of a dick throbbing inside you, and feeling that man's energy mesh with mine. Feeling his power, and tasting his sweat..." she said, somewhat dreamily.

None of that shit sounded the least bit appealing to me, but I couldn't knock her for what she'd done or how she lived her life before we met.

"So are you asking me for permission to cheat?" I countered.

"That's not what I'm saying. I'm just asking how this is supposed to go because it all happened so sudden, and I didn't expect to swear off dick forever when I met you."

"Well, then we probably should've had this conversation in Vegas, but to answer your question, I don't see a way that dick fits into our life unless you're cheating. And if THAT happens, then you better pray I never find out about it," I warned seriously.

"Okay, so then how do you expect one of us to get pregnant?" she countered logically.

"The good old-fashioned way, as in with a turkey baster and someone's donation in a cup."

I could still feel her staring at me, but no words came from between her lips. I hadn't meant for this to turn into a fight, just a conversation between spouses about the life we planned to build moving forward. It was clear that it didn't matter what my intentions were though because we were here now, and I had to be careful because I didn't wanna say something that I couldn't take back.

"Listen, Kali, I'm not trying to be unreasonable, it's just that—"

The sound of her phone pinging in her hand halted my statement, and when I looked over, it was clear that her attention was elsewhere. That was okay though, and I'd let this go for now, but not forever.

"Babe, stop the car," Kali said suddenly.

"What?"

"I said STOP the car," she repeated, still reading from the phone's screen.

"What's up?" I asked, pulling onto the side of the road quickly.

"It's my mom. She needs my help or she's gonna die - and not by Leroy's hand."

# CHAPTER 16

*Leroy*

"Y-you went after my family?" Zuk stammered, still staring at my phone's screen as if he was in a trance.

"They're not supposed to be more family than I am, BROTHER, and you came after ME, so that should make us about even," I replied, still smiling.

As if on cue, I saw Matt coming out of the kitchen, and our eyes immediately locked. His subtle nod gave me even more confidence than the phone in my hand, and I quickly formulated a plan of action.

"Why don't we take this conversation outside where we can get some fresh air and let cooler heads prevail?" I suggested, standing up.

I could tell by the slightly glazed look in Zuk's eyes that part of him was lost as to what he should do in this situation. He was a killer himself and had plenty of blood on his hands, but he knew firsthand just how ruthless I could be when pushed. After all, it had been him that had to clean up the mess I'd made of my own daughter and her boyfriend, so there was little hope in him when it came to me sparing his family. His options were limited, and that was a drastic turn of events considering the supreme confidence he'd walked into my restaurant with.

"Get up Zuk," I said, feeling no sympathy for his emotional plight.

"L, listen, it wasn't my idea to come at you like this, and you gotta know that. Come on, bruh, let my family go and we'll go our separate ways right now," he pleaded, rising shakily to his feet.

I laughed in his face as I put my phone in my pocket and started walking towards the kitchen.

"Is everything okay? My people are out back waiting on my signal," Matt said when I got close enough to hear him speaking in low tones.

"We're good. Come on," I replied, motioning for him to turn around and retrace his steps. I didn't have to look behind me to know that Zuk was following me because I was holding all the cards in this situation, but now the question on my mind was, how did I want to play it? When we stepped outside the back of the restaurant, I pulled up short at the sight of two military Hummers parked a few feet away with eight heavily-armed white men standing in front of them with their guns at the ready. It looked like a military exercise was about to take place right here in my parking lot.

"Tell your men to stand down for a few minutes while I try to resolve this diplomatically," I said.

While Matt went to do that, I focused my attention on Zuk and the Rulers he'd brought with him.

"Do your men know who I am?" I asked all six men standing with Zuk.

They looked around amongst each other, but they were all shaking their heads in a negative motion.

"Why don't you tell these prospects who I am, Zuk. Tell them just how far loyalty goes inside the Nation of Rulers," I said.

The look of discomfort on Zuk's face was as easy to read as the  sign on top of my restaurant, but I felt nothing for this man that I'd considered a brother and friend for so many years.

"This man is one of the founding fathers of the Nation of Rulers," Zuk replied finally.

"And why does IG wanna see me bad enough to send you after me like I was some nobody on the street?" I asked, forcing him to explain the mission these men had blindly engaged in.

"To remove your patch as a 1%er," Zuk said.

"For what crime have I committed against a Ruler, or what law have I broken within the bylaws of Ruler Nation?" I asked persistently.

"I-I don't know," Zuk mumbled.

"You were doing so good at telling the truth, so don't start lying now, my nigga," I warned.

For a moment, Zuk just stared at me, and in that look, I could see understanding for what I was doing in the moment. This was a learning experience, but it was also the beginning of my campaign to assume complete leadership of the Nation of Rulers worldwide.

"It’s okay, bruh, you can tell them the truth, and it'll set you free. They deserve to hear it, and to know exactly how the previous leadership did things in the name of being a supreme Ruler," I said.

Even as I was speaking the truth, utter defeat took over Zuk's facial features, and he looked like a shell of himself.

"Y-you have not committed any crime against a Ruler or the Nation, nor have you broken any bylaws. IG wants your patch because he can't control you anymore, and that makes him fear you," Zuk admitted.

"So that would make his actions, and yours, acts of treason, wouldn't it?" I asked.

"It would," Zuk agreed.

"Prospects, what is the penalty for treason?" I asked.

The men looked at each other again, and it was clear that all of them knew the answer, but nobody really wanted to say it.

"Death," someone finally said.

"That's right, the penalty for treason is death, gentlemen, and NOBODY is bigger than the laws of the Nation. I'm not an unreasonable man, nor do I lack mercy completely, so I'll give you a chance, Zuk. I can put a bullet in your brain, and then tell my man to kill your family just to send my message. Or, you can take your own life, and in return, I'll spare your family the fate of death right now. I learned this from watching the *Godfather Part 2*," I said, smiling.

"Y-you want me to k-kill myself?" he asked in disbelief.

"That's EXACTLY what I want you to do, and I want you to appreciate the beauty in taking your own life in sacrifice of the ones you love. It's your last chance to demonstrate true loyalty, which means this is your last chance to balance the scales of karma before it's too late. The big picture is that this is your last day on earth regardless, and the next thirty seconds will decide what the dash in between your birth date and death date on your headstone stood for," I replied, pulling my pistol out.

All eyes were on Zuk, but his eyes were closed as he either tried to make peace with his demons of the past or get acquainted with the demons in his future. Maybe it was both. I was silently counting in my mind and I got all the way to 15 Mississippi before his eyes slowly opened and he looked directly at me. One might confuse the water in his eyes with an allergy problem on this nice day, but I knew different, and I saw his fear of the unknown swimming in the depths of those waters. It took another five seconds for him to pull his pistol out from the waist of his jeans, and his motion made the young wolves take a step backwards out of instinctive reflex.

"Y-you promise that my family lives?" Zuk mumbled through his tears.

"I give you my word as a Supreme Ruler," I replied sincerely.

He nodded sadly and took a couple of deep breaths. Up until this point, he seemed to be moving in slow motion, but that changed when he swiftly raised his gun to his head and pulled the trigger. The cannon roared and breathed fire against his temple as his brains were pushed aside like uneaten mashed potatoes in the same direction that his body tipped and crumbled.

For a few seconds I just stared at him, absorbing the lifeless look in his eyes and etching it into my memory with a hammer and a chisel. For the first time in years, I actually thought about Cyn's mom and how she'd taken her life because I wouldn't forgive her. All these years later, I was still that same person, so what had I actually learned? I didn't know. All I knew was to keep pushing because there were no roads leading back to whence I came. I put my pistol away and pulled my phone back out, immediately sending a text to Phantom with instructions for his people to let Zuk's family go unharmed because they'd served their purpose. The next thing I did was take two pictures of Zuk's body, and I sent them to IG with two words attached: I'm coming.

"Each of you prospects, give me your driver's licenses," I demanded, holding my hand out.

One by one they stepped forward, and I took a picture of their licenses before returning them and then dismissing them all with instructions to tell others what they'd learned here today. When I turned to go to Matt, I caught the look of astonishment on the faces of him and his men, but I chose to ignore them because we had bigger issues. I motioned for him to meet me at my bike so that my words wouldn't be overhead by people who didn't need to hear them.

"I know that was crazy, but we got other shit to worry about. That was a message sent, so I fired one back, but we both know it doesn't stop there. We're at war, and I need your help."

"You've got it. Just tell me what you need."

"I need this called in anonymously because I need to get to Erin and make sure she's good before I have to disappear for a while. I need you to make sure she's good no matter what happens, like we discussed," I replied.

"I got you. Now get going, and tell my sister I love her."

We half-hugged before I hopped on my bike and took off. My mind was racing, but I felt no panic or fear, because while I may have been a businessman by title, I was forever a warrior at heart. I was battle tested and ready to fuck a nigga's day up, whenever, wherever.

By the time I pulled up outside Dana's cabin in Kentucky, darkness had descended over the day, robbing me of some of my eyesight, but welcoming the new moon with open arms. From a mile out, I could spot the presence of Dana's chapter of the Nation of Rulers posted like sentries amongst the trees and showing their allegiance to me in this war. It made me miss Dana, but it also fueled my desire to do right by all she'd cared about, because she'd sacrificed it all to ride with me.

"Erin?" I called, coming into the cabin.

She appeared instantly from around a corner, and the relief on her face was as instant as it was evident.

"Matt called and told me that you were coming, but it felt like it was taking forever for you to get here."

"I'm sorry, baby. I used the open road to try and clear my head in preparation of what's coming," I replied.

"I understand. Matt told me what happened."

When I looked at her quizzically, she reached behind her back and pulled out a sexy Walther .22 with a ridiculous banana clip attached to it.

"What the FUCK is that?" I asked, impressed.

"It's a .22 that holds 50 rounds. You can't forget that I'm Matt's sister, and I've been shooting shit since I was knee high to a grasshopper. I will protect my family, you, and our unborn child until the bitter end, just like I know you will," she replied passionately.

I pulled her into my arms for a tender, yet passionate kiss, and just held her for a few minutes while the world moved around us. I needed this calm in the storm, because even though I knew I'd have to stand on business and get active with these niggas coming for me, I didn't want get lost in the bloodlust. It was important to remain grounded, or risk losing myself forever.

'I've missed you," I whispered against her soft lips.

"Oh really? Do you wanna show me how much, since it could be a while before we're alone like this again?"

My response was to scoop her up into my arms and carry her into the spare bedroom we'd been utilizing. I laid her down gently and took the gun from her hand, sliding it up under the pillow with my own. From there, we took our time undressing each other, making each touch and kiss as sensual as it would forever be memorable. The suspense of the seduction had the air circulating in a limited way, but the heat between us was embraced as we laid together in our naked glory. I let her take control, and she rolled me on my back while taking my hard dick inside her warm, slippery walls with an obvious hunger that matched my own. From that moment, I lost all train of thought, and I was willingly lost to her supreme powers.

# CHAPTER 17

*Lia*

"Let me read the message for myself," I said, holding my hand out for her phone.

When she passed it to me, I read the short text that said IG was gonna kill Gini, and that he'd kidnapped her.

"We know that she willingly got on that bike with IG though, just like she's willingly been complicit in manipulating my dad from the jump. How do we know that she's telling the truth? Because this could be a setup," I said.

"I know all of that, Lia, but this just FEELS true. I don't know why IG would suddenly flip the script on her, but you have to admit that their motivations are different. IG wants to destroy your dad, and my mom just wants him all to herself with no outside interference."

I couldn't deny the truth in that statement, but I still wasn't ready to drink the Kool-Aid and just believe that her mom was suddenly the damsel in distress. Asking me to swallow that was like suggesting I put a down payment on the Brooklyn Bridge.

"We need to call my dad either way," I said, passing her phone back and pulling out my own.

I quickly dialed my dad's number and listened to it ring ten times before I hung up and called right back. When I got the same results, I swore softly under my breath, dropped the truck into drive, and pulled off fast back into traffic. The sound of car horns was immediate, clearly angry with both me and Benji because he was riding my bumper.

"We gotta get in touch with my dad and put together a workable plan. Trying to go at IG halfcocked could get us or your mom killed, so we need to get to Kentucky and regroup, " I said, pushing the pedal to the floor.

"Give me your phone so that I can keep trying to call your dad while I text my mom and find out all I can."

I passed her my phone, but my eyes never left the road in front of me. It was a full three hours later when we slid to a stop in front of Dana's cabin, with nothing short of ten guns aimed at us from various angles. Benji hopped out of his truck and all guns immediately went down, which allowed me and Kali to get out without fear of getting shot. Benji met us at the front of my truck.

"My people say that your dad is here and he's been here for hours, but the lights have been off inside for a while. Maybe they're just asleep," he said.

"It would explain why he didn't answer his phone," Kali said.

"Fuck the guessing shit. We're here now," I said, heading for the cabin door.

Out of reflex, I pulled my pistol and banged on the door like NY foot was seconds away from rendering the locks and deadbolts useless. I didn't get an answer fast enough, so I started banging again, and then lights came on in the interior of the cabin. I didn't realize I was holding my breath until it was released in a sudden whoosh, like a pressure release valve. When the door was snatched open, I saw my dad standing there with his pistol raised high, looking more menacing than a scary movie.

"Um, damn," Kali said under her breath.

It wasn't until then that I noticed my dad was butt-ass naked.

"Dad, put some clothes on," I demanded, stepping in front of Kali to obscure her view.

"Why the fuck are you banging on the door like that, girl? Are you crazy?" he asked, more than a little pissed.

"I'm sorry. There's a lot going on, and we've been calling you for the past three hours with no answer," I explained.

"What's going on, L?" Erin asked, walking up beside him.

It became real clear why our calls had gone unanswered.

"Um, damn," Kali said louder, peeking around me to see Erin's body.

"Will you two please put some clothes on," I said, pushing the gun in my father's hand down.

"You two go sit on the couch," my dad instructed, taking Erin by the hand and leading her back down the hall into the bedroom.

"Put your eyes back in your damn head and come on," I said, leading the way inside the cabin.

"You can't possibly get mad at me for looking at naked people. That's like driving past a car accident and not rubbernecking to see what you can see," Kali replied, laughing softly.

"Just get focused, will you?" I said.

"You're right. I haven't heard from my mom again, so let's just hope your dad can put together the pieces of the puzzle."

We sat in silence and waited for my dad, each of us analyzing our own thoughts individually and trying to figure out the next move. When he came back in the room a few minutes, later he had some sweatpants on, but he was still shirtless, and he had his phone in his hand.

"Dad, Kali got a text message from her mom saying that she needs help because IG is gonna kill her. I don't know if it's true because we know—"

"You know nothing," he said, not looking up from his phone.

"Huh?" I replied, confused by his curtness.

"I said, you know nothing. But don't worry about it. I'll take care of it," he said.

"So it's true?" Kali asked.

Her question forced him to look up from his phone's screen and look her directly in the eyes. He paused briefly before responding, but I could feel what was coming.

"It's true. IG is holding your mom as leverage, banking on the fact that I MIGHT love her still and be willing to negotiate a truce. Right now he's feeling the pressure because I've got his secret army under attack, which makes them useless to him, and the word is swiftly spreading throughout the Nation of Rulers that he's committing treason. He's about to lose everything."

"I know that the shit my mom did was unnecessary, wrong, and stupid, but Leroy, you can't let him kill her. Please," Kali pleaded emotionally.

"Of course I can let IG kill her, because then I don't have to do it my damn self," he replied dispassionately.

"So you don't love her anymore? Just like that?" Kali asked, rising to her feet angrily.

As if on cue, Erin came from out of the back bedroom fully dressed with a pistol in a holster on her hip in plain view. She walked over to stand beside my dad, and I said a silent prayer that Kali wouldn't escalate the situation.

"Of course Leroy still loves Gini, but has he not given her enough? Has he not risked his life enough for her?" Erin asked calmly.

"I didn't know I was talking to YOU," Kali said sarcastically, clearly not backing down.

I could tell by the look on Erin's face that she wasn't one to back down either, which meant some type of compromise was needed because this shit show wasn't solving anything.

"Dad, would you leave Erin at the mercy of a madman?" I asked, rising to my feet.

His eyes swung in my direction, and I knew he understood the point I was making. Real loyalty came with qualifications, but if that's who you were at your core, then you had to stay true to that or risk losing yourself. Undoubtedly, we'd all agree that my dad didn't owe Gini shit, but her dying at the hands of a nigga she wouldn't have come into contact with without my dad would always weigh on his soul.

"I wouldn't do the things Gini did, but I get your point somewhat, Lia. What I don't think either of you is getting is the fact that I'm pregnant with Leroy's child. He didn't get to raise you or your sister, and you know how much that hurt you both. Would you want your next sibling to go through that?"

It was on the tip of my tongue to tell Erin FUCK her goddamn baby and question its paternity along the way because she was definitely still married, but I chose the high road of understanding.

"I wouldn't wish that pain on anyone, but whether you like it or not, Gini is family, and we don't leave family for dead. Do we...Dad?" I asked pointedly.

All eyes turned towards him because this one question was one of character to the man standing before us. It reminded me of something Leroy had told me a long time ago. He'd said it cost him nothing to be real, but it could cost him everything if he's not. This situation would surely test that theory.

Suddenly, Kali was moving towards him, and she didn't stop until she was standing in front of him, toe to toe, looking up into his eyes.

"I know you're a businessman, so how about we barter a favor for a favor? All I'm asking is that you save her life. I'm not saying that you two will love happily ever after, nor does you saving her mean that she's forgiven. Just look it like any other business transaction," Kali reasoned.

I didn't understand the look that she and him shared, but I noticed that he didn't say no immediately, which was a positive sign. Kali motioned for him to lean down to her so that she could say something on his ear and he complied, but his expression remained neutral. After a few moments he pulled back and looked at Erin before looking back to Kali. He and Kali continued their silent communication, but then he looked to Erin again and took her hand in his.

"IG has control of an entire apartment complex in the south side of Richmond, and he's barricaded inside. He sent me an invitation to come sit down with him, assuring me that we could work through our differences," he said.

"Do you believe him?" I asked.

"Of course not. The only way for IG to remain on the throne now is to kill me, along with everyone who would think about avenging me. In his former GD gang life, it's called a Blackout."

"Do you think he can pull it off?" Kali asked.

"I think the most dangerous animal is the one that's cornered," he replied.

"What do we do, Dad?"

When his moved back to lock eyes with mine, I saw steel burning within his iris, and it caused me to involuntarily shiver with fear. Before my very eyes the man, the myth, and the legend were merging to create a threat I didn't think IG or anybody else wanted to see come their way. Depending on what happened in the end, I knew I might regret convincing the monster inside my father to come out one last time, but I couldn't think about it right now. In this moment, the devil was needed, and I was okay with calling him forward because I knew it was the only way for me to survive too.

"Lia, you and Kali need to do what I tell you, when I tell you. No questions asked," he stated.

"Understood," Kali replied readily.

I nodded in agreement.

"I don't need either of you on the front line with me right now. I need you protecting our family instead. Lia, I want both of you to go to your grandmother's house and get her and Candice. Bring them back here for safe keeping. You all will be protected here by Rulers that are loyal to me, plus the security people that are on the payroll."

"What about you, Dad? Won't that leave you vulnerable? You can't possibly plan to go on IG's territory all by yourself."

"That's what it'll seem like, but trust me when I tell you that I'm never alone, and I damn sure ain't nobody's fool. IG ain't negotiating from a position of power, and if he wasn't so desperate, he'd see that."

"What do you mean?" Kali asked.

"He's trying to tap into my emotions and get me to make a decision based on that, but he knows I'm not that type of nigga. His desperation, along with the blind loyalty I showed Gini, has him convinced that I'll still go to the ends of the earth for her."

"So what are you gonna do, Dad?"

"I'm gonna do the only thing I can do. I'm gonna bring hell to earth."

# CHAPTER 18

*Leroy*

*Next day*

My eyes burned from looking at the tiny lines on my phone's screen for the past few hours, but it had been necessary to study the blueprints for the apartment complex IG had control of. I needed to analyze every point of weakness before taking a run at IG's stronghold because only a fool, or a bat, would fly blind. So far, I didn't like what I was seeing because there was no way to truly contain the scene without a lot of manpower. With this thought in mind, I texted my nigga 2 so I could find out how many niggas he had in Virginia that I could take into battle with me. While I waited on his reply, I texted my own chapter of Rulers and let them know our destination, along with the time we would ride out to Richmond. I'd only chosen the men that I could say with absolute certainty that I trusted with my life because that knife coming from behind was always the deadliest.

"Ayo slim, I gotta step out and handle some business. You gonna be good?" Noodles asked, coming into the living room.

"Yeah, I'm straight, bruh. I'll hit you up if anything changes."

"A'ight, my nigga," he said, turning to leave.

Noodles would've went to war with me had I asked him to, but instead, I'd just asked him for a place to lay low until it was time to shake shit. Him owning the entire apartment complex gave me a feeling of safety and allowed me to blend in undetected. Hiding forever wasn't an option or the plan, so I shifted my mind back to the strategical stage of the battle before me. I'd been up most of the night trying to visualize and strategize the perfect way to end IG's life, but he was a worthy adversary, and he was slippery as fuck too. I knew that he'd undoubtedly be trying to predict my moves because he knew me so well, which meant I'd have to do something he wouldn't see coming. Right at this moment, I didn't know what that was, but it was definitely outside of the box where I'd find it.

If me and my team rushed his hood in a full-on blitz attack, there was little doubt in my mind that he'd kill Gini just out of spite, and that's what I was trying to avoid. My heart was torn when it came to saving her, but I was still thinking clearly when it came to planning. What I really needed was a shooter that could hit the target from a mile out, and the only person I knew who had those type of guys was the military. I immediately texted Matt to see if he and any buddies fitting this specific qualification, and then I was back to waiting impatiently. It was no fun being by myself, but I took comfort in the fact that those that I loved the most were safely hidden in Kentucky. I couldn't guarantee victory, so I was gonna approach the situation with caution when it came to my family's vulnerability. Thinking of them now had me ready to send a text, but suddenly, my phone started ringing in my hand. I didn't recognize the number, so I started not to answer it, but something inside me pushed back against that thought.

"Hello?" I said cautiously.

"IG just left Creighton Court apartments in a 50-bike battalion headed to Washington, D.C. to sit down with the Department of Justice and testify against you. He has incriminating evidence to link you to the attack on Fluvana prison, and if you let him make it to that meeting, the feds will hunt you to the ends of the earth. You gotta stop him, L. Your wife is in the black van travelling behind the bikes. She's alive, but beaten badly. Thought is Ruler."

"And Ruler is supreme," I replied.

The phone went dead in my ear, and for a second, I thought that I'd imagined the whole conversation. The caller hadn't said their name, but the voice was familiar enough for me to know that it was as Ruler member. Besides recognizing the voice, the words they spoke about IG's plan had a ring of truth to them because it was the one move I hadn't anticipated. I'd been expecting IG to fight fair, or at least fight by the code of the streets, but at this point, there were no rules, and if IG had his way there would only be ONE supreme Ruler.

Reality flashing before my eyes kicked my fingers I to gear, and the first thing I did was shoot Matt a text message. It took an hour and a half to two hours to get from Richmond to D.C. if you were doing the speed limit, and considering that he had kidnapped a woman he was about to traffic across state lines, I expected him to do the speed limit. Mentally, that gave me an hour to formulate a plan and assemble the welcome party for his traitorous ass. I sent a text to Phantom and 2 after my text to Matt because this was the time to go all in on this situation like there was no tomorrow. Matt hit me right back and asked me what I needed. I could feel the smile on my face as I sent the answer back to him. I waited patiently to see what he'd say, and after a few minutes, my phone finally pinged with a two-word reply. “Let's play.” I hopped up off the couch I'd been sitting on and headed for the front door. It only took me a minute to jump on my bike and have it growling loudly as I flew out of the parking lot. I headed to Boiling Air Force Base, which was a short drive across the Woodrow Wilson bridge, and then a drop down to I-295.

Within fifteen minutes, I was at the south entrance to the base, waiting on Matt to come to the front. I checked my phone to find messages from Phantom and 2, asking me where I needed their men to be and when I needed them there. I knew there a few routes from Richmond into D.C., but my money was on them taking route 64 to route 81 because given the number of bikes travelling, I doubted they'd take any back roads. The best place to hit them was when they got off 81 and hopped on I-395, which would spill them into the mixing bowl outside of Springfield. I instructed him to have his men go straight to the Springfield mixing bowl, and I'd meet them there. By the time I sent that message, I spotted Matt at the guard post waving me through, and I eased my bike forward onto the base. I pulled over to the side in a parking space that was reserved for vehicle searches, and I waited for Matt.

"You're gonna have to go from here straight to the rendezvous point because the helicopter is getting ready to take off. It's two 60mm machine guns on each side with gunners manning them, and their instructions are to shoot wherever you point this laser," he said, passing me something that looked like an expensive ink pen.

I studied it just to make sure that I knew how to use it, and then I put it in my pocket.

"Thanks bruh, I really appreciate it."

"It's nothing, and we shall never speak of it. If you need anything else, just let me know," he replied.

I nodded and then I put my bike in gear and turned around to get off base. As soon as I cleared the gate, I had my bike up on its rear wheel for damn near half a mile before I put it down and really got moving. With expert maneuvering, and no fear for death, I pushed my bike to its limits on every straight stretch I could find. A little less than half an hour later, I pulled up to a stop in the Holiday Inn parking lot in Springfield. I calmly walked inside like any other patron and paid for a two-night stay while requesting to be on the twelfth floor. After paying for my room and getting my keycard, I took the elevator up. I went to my room and put the do not disturb sign on the door. The first thing that I did was open the curtains and check the view, and I was excited to see that I and a clear shot of the mixing bowl below.

I quickly sent Phantom a message and told him to have his men post up on the side of the road right by the on ramp to go to D.C. and wait for my next text. When I sent that, it would be the signal for them to get ready, because as soon as IG got onto the highway, I wanted him boxed in. The boys in the air would do the rest. With the plans in motion, all I could do now was wait, and while I did that, I decided to send Erin a text message. There was no doubt in my mind that after this, we were gonna have to leave the country, so I wanted her to get a head start on planning our escape. I left our final destination up to her while promising that she'd always be able to come back for her boys because my goal wasn't to take her from them. She was a part of my life now, and it was what we both wanted, so why not embrace it? I still had to talk to her about what it meant to be polygamous, by ultimately, I didn't think she would mind.

When my phone pinged in my hand, I was expecting the text to be from Erin, but it wasn't. It was from an unknown number, and the message was a hotel room number and location with two words on it, “for later”, attached to it. My confusion evaporated quickly as I played back a conversation I'd had not long ago, but I pushed that from my mind as the faint sound of a helicopter reached my ears. My eyes immediately went to the sky, and I spotted the beautiful black bird in the distance hovering over top of the mixing bowl. I put my phone on the window sill and I pulled the laser out. All I needed now was to look out the window and see the predator.

# CHAPTER 19

*Leroy*

Anticipation was building in my chest along with excitement, because I wanted to see how this shit was gonna play out. A quick text to Phantom told him and his people that Gini was riding in a black Ford Econoline panel van, and it was now travelling in the middle of the fifty bikes currently headed in their direction. I'd already spotted IG riding out in front of the pack, but he wasn't moving with the speed of somebody being chased or hunted, which meant that he didn't know I was on his ass yet. Knowing him, he probably thought I was still oblivious to his fuckery, and he felt like the crown was already secure on his head. I couldn't wait for him to feel the truth. They were only about a mile from the on ramp they'd need to merge onto, but a red light brought them to a standstill. An impulsive decision had me pick my phone back up and call IG's phone, because I knew that his Bluetooth was connected to his helmet. It rang twice and then the rough gravel of his voice came through my phone's speaker.

"What the fuck do you want?" he asked angrily.

"For you to watch your tone, and remember who the fuck you're talking to, nigga. I'm only coming to sit down with you as a courtesy because I really should just KILL your muthafuckin' ass."

"Yeah, well if you were as smart as you think you are, nigga, then you would've killed me. It's too late now though. You played your hand wrong, and now I'm the Suge Knight of this shit," he gloated, laughing.

I heard his bike accelerate as he pulled off from the light, and it made me smile as I fingered the laser in my hand.

"Too late? Oh, so you don't want me to come meet with you? You don't want me to spare your miserable fucking life, PUSSY?" I asked.

"Fuck you, BITCH! You're already dead because I've got a bigger mob behind me now, and it's called the United States Government versus Leroy Bly! Let me know what the food is like when you get to ADX Florence supermax prison in Colorado."

His laughter rang out loud and clear over the line, and I could tell he was enjoying it because of the self-satisfaction in his melody.

"You WOULD think that you could outsmart me, wouldn't you? I've got bad news for you, Mr. Infinite Gangster. You could NEVER outsmart me. Since you wanted to be Suge Knight so bad, my nigga, WELCOME TO DEATH ROW! You're dead right about now," I said, aiming the laser out the window and putting the beam squarely on his predator helmet.

I tracked his movements with the laser as I saw the helicopter suddenly drop out of the sky like it was malfunctioning. Before he could reach the top of the on ramp, the bright day turned into a Hollywood light show, and bullets rained from the sky. Within seconds, IG was shredded, headless, and no more, so I kept moving the laser down the line of bikes behind him. Before I knew it, the scene unfolding outside my window was a drive-by shooting that was historical in its invention. The bikes and riders that weren't obliterated by the helicopter ran smack into another wall of gunfire from the ground support when they tried to backtrack. Their coffin was sealed in less than three minutes, and once I saw Gini removed from the van, I put the laser away. The light show ended and the helicopter took back to the skies like it had never been there, leaving behind the bloodstains, brain fragments, and human intestines on the usually quiet suburban streets. I stood at the window for a few more seconds admiring the massacre before texting Phantom the next location for his people to meet me so that I could get Gini back. I waited a while before taking the elevator back downstairs and going around to the hotel's rear entrance.

Within a few minutes, a black and blue 2028 Dodge Charger pulled up and Gini climbed from the front seat looking like a stray puppy in from the cold. I could tell that she was slightly disoriented, and I could see the cuts, bruises, and swelling on her face and arms. When our eyes locked though, my stomach dropped, and suddenly I was more confused than I'd ever been. She didn't speak a word. She simply moved towards me and took a leap of faith by stepping into my arms. I held her out of instinct as my mind flashed back to the many times we'd spent together like this during prison visitation. I'd always thought that we'd have more years in front of us than behind us, but for so many reasons, I knew that was no longer true - the biggest one being that I hated her as much as I loved her. I broke our embrace by taking a step back, turning to lead the way back upstairs to my room. We didn't hold hands, but her presence and closeness were felt, especially once we were on the elevator. The silence as we rode up was thick and awkward, but I honestly didn't care enough to try to smooth things over, for real. Her being here was business as far as I was concerned.

"You can take a shower and I'll order you some food, but we've gotta get back on the road sooner rather than later," I said once we were inside the hotel room.

"Are you joining me in the shower?"

"Are you trying to be funny?" I asked, giving her a look of pure disgust.

"I was actually being serious because I missed you, but the way you're looking at me is like you think my pussy is full of semen from ten different men, and you want no part of it. Just so you know, NOBODY touched me in that way, Leroy."

"That's not why I looked at you like that. I looked at you like you don't deserve this dick, or any other part of me, so why the fuck should I give it to you?"

"How about because I'm your WIFE! I know that I fucked up and made some dumb-ass decisions, but after ALL that we've been through, I would think that I deserve a second chance. I swear that I never meant to hurt you Leroy. I just wanted you so bad that I got scared of losing you."

"Then I guess it's ironic, because instead of the shit you doing bringing us closer, it actually destroyed us. I gave you everything I had! I gave you your fucking freedom, and your life back! Was that not enough?" I asked, fighting the emotions trying to take me over the edge.

"All I ever wanted was all of you, Leroy. Was that too much to ask?"

As absurd as her question sounded, I actually understood what she meant. This whole time I'd thought that she'd been a willing participant in my polygamous lifestyle, but it was really something I'd forced on her. I hadn't asked for her opinion, I'd just told her that this was what it is, and she could take it or leave it. I know that I wouldn't have gone to the extremes that she did to have me all to herself, but I know I wouldn't have accepted her fucking other niggas. Somebody would've had to die, and probably her too.

"Why didn't you ever say anything about my lifestyle if you wanted to be in a monogamous relationship?" I asked.

"Because I didn't want that to be the reason we couldn't be together. I figured that having some of you was better than having none of you, and for a while, I convinced myself of that, but...I knew that once I came home, I'd just being lying to myself and becoming bitter for it because the reality was that I wanted it all. I wanted all of you."

"You didn't feel that way about me being with Dana though," I pointed out.

"You're right, I didn't, but that was because Dana was a decision that we made together as a couple, and not something I was forced to accept. Plus, she didn't wanna be a sister wife. She just wanted to have fun."

"I just don't understand why you couldn't talk to me about all of this, Gini. I mean, I've always heard you out before."

"I was scared," she replied simply.

I didn't have a ready response to that honest admission because I knew from personal experience that the only emotion more powerful than hope is fear. Fear could paralyze any man or woman, it didn't discriminate, and I knew it wasn't as simple as telling someone to get over it. If I was being honest with myself, then I had to admit the part that I played in the problems between her and me, but didn't know where to find the words to begin explaining.

As if sensing this, Gini suddenly reached her hand out to me, and held it there for me to take. When I looked into her eyes, I saw so much understanding and forgiveness that I felt overwhelmed by my own now-surging emotions. After fighting with myself for several seconds, I reached out and joined my hand to hers. Without a word she led me to the bathroom, and turned the shower on. As the steam quickly built, she turned to face me and slowly began to take her clothes off without taking her eyes away from mine.

I felt a moment of hesitation when she started to push my shirt up over my head, but I let her continue while lifting my arms. She dropped the shirt to the floor and pulled my gun free from my jeans before she set it on the sink so that she could go for my jeans. She had them at my ankles within seconds, followed immediately by my boxer briefs, both of which I stepped out of willingly, already warming up to the naughty ideas swimming in her eyes. The way that she eased down to her knees was a sensual seduction on display as she looked up at me submissively and then took my dick fully into her mouth. The back of her throat possessed the same heat and snug feeling that I could never forget, and by the time she walked her lips back up my shaft, my dick was throbbing like a boxer's speed bag. I could feel my heart beating through my lower anatomy. Part of me wanted to just admire her work, but it was impossible for me to keep this intense staring contest as she ate my dick over and over again without cumming. I could hear my knees bang together like a Crip in a Blood neighborhood, and at that point, it was only my pride that kept me upright. The fire in her eyes told me that she was trying to bend me to her will, and that made me resist more.

I grabbed a fistful of her hair and fucked her face to the brink of spilling my seed down her throat in a wild rush, but I stopped short. With my hand still gripping her hair, I pulled her to her feet and marched her into the hot shower until her back hit the tile wall. I spun her around, adjusting my grip on her hair, and plowed my dick up into her hot pussy hard enough to lift her feet off the ground. I kept her pinned to the wall under my steady long strokes, forcing her to swallow the shower's steam as she cried out in ecstasy. Her pussy grip was like a vice, but I fought it until it accepted the punishment I was giving and it squeezed me lovingly in return. Within moments, I could feel the torrential rain coming down in the form of her cumming on my dick, and only then did I let her down off the wall. I spun her back around and used the hand still on her head to guide her back to her knees. She opened her mouth wide for me, and then she locked my dick back inside her jaws like it was a bank vault. I didn't even try to resist this time, I just raised my hands high in the air and let her do what she did best. In under two minutes I was shooting cum at the back of her throat like a sprinkler head watering a baseball field, and she drank every drop of it. She sucked my dick until I was forced to brace myself against the shower wall or fall flat on my back. When she finally released me, it was with a self-satisfied smile on her face, and a twinkle of mischief in her eyes. I'd seen that look before, so I knew that it meant that she intended for this to be the beginning of a sexual marathon, but I wasn't mentally or emotionally ready for that. I'd been a willing participant in everything that had just taken place, but the guilt was already starting to set in, and all I could see was Erin in my mind's eye. To make it worse, I knew that I'd just fucked Gini with Erin's pussy, mouth, and ass still on my dick from our reunion at the cabin. This guilt was foreign to me, and it fucked with my mind so much that I suddenly felt claustrophobic in the shower.

"I'm g-gonna order some food," I said lamely, making a speedy exit out into the bedroom after scooping up my clothes and gun.

I dressed rapidly, and then I ordered a couple burgers with fries to the room. While I waited on the delivery, I pulled my phone out and sent a text to Lia so that she could let everyone know that all was well and it was finally over. I told her that we'd be on the road shortly. By the time that was done, Gini was coming out of the bathroom beautifully naked with a towel in her hands, drying her hair.

"You know, L, based on what just happened in there, I think you lied to me when you didn't admit that you missed me too."

"You're funny," I replied.

"No, I'm serious. You haven't fucked me like that since I first came home, but I like how you handled me rough."

I didn't respond. I just kept my eyes on my phone's screen and my ears were listening for the knock at the door.

"Why are you acting weird, bae? Aren't we good now, or at least in a better place than when we came in this room?" she asked, sitting next to me on the bed.

There were several different ways to answer that question, but in my heart, I knew only the truth had a place in this moment.

"I need to tell you something, Gini."

"You can tell me anything, L. I love you."

"You won't after I tell you this...because I got Erin pregnant."

# Chapter 20

*Lia*

I felt like I'd been checking the time on my phone every five minutes since my dad texted me and said that he had Gini back and IG was dead. He'd said it was all over now, but something in the pit of my stomach was bothering me. At first, I'd thought that it was just the fact that my uncertain future was now the next mountain to climb and I hadn't a clue on how to scale it. But now I was thinking that it was more than that. I trusted my instincts religiously, and right now, there was unseen danger that we were blind to.

"Hey Erin?" I called out.

When she came in the living room from the kitchen, I quickly scrutinized her, but nothing about her seemed off or out of place.

"Yeah Lia?"

"Have you heard from my dad?"

"No, but I didn't expect to hear from him. Isn't he on his way back here?"

"Yeah, that's what he said a couple hours ago," I replied.

"Then he's on his bike, which is why he's not answering if you called or texted him. I've had to go through that same shit, waiting anxiously, and then he'll suddenly appear. If I didn't know, I'd think he does shit like that for dramatic effect," she said, chuckling and shaking her head as she went back into the kitchen.

"I've got a couple of ideas of how we can past the time," Kali said, smiling at me from her seat beside me on the couch.

I rolled my eyes at her and went back to staring at my phone to keep from going off on her silly ass.

"Lia, you've been giving me the cold shoulder since your dad left, but not once have you put on your big girl panties and told me what the fuck is really bothering you."

"Big girl panties? I tried to have a conversation with you, but you shut that shit down real quick," I replied with growing frustration.

"No, you didn't try to have a conversation. You tried to interrogate me, OFFICER Panel."

"It wasn't a fucking interrogation, Kali. I just asked you what the fuck you whispered in my dad's ear!"

"And that's my point! You're asking me questions that the chick who's sucking and fucking him ain't asking. Obviously, whatever I said to him was just for him and me, or I would've said the shit out loud," she replied, matching my heated energy.

"How the fuck does it look that my wife has secrets with MY dad?"

"Calm down, because he's only been DADDY to you for a New York minute, and you know it. You wanted to kill the man, and now you act like you're his pretty princess who has to protect him. Where the fuck do they do that at?"

"South side Richmond is where we do that at, and if you keep bumping your dick suckers, I'ma show you what that means," I threatened.

"Well, I'm from Star City, sweetheart, and that shit ain't on me; it's in me. I ain't never been scared of no bitch or taking no fade, so I suggest you put them threats in your pussy!"

Before I knew it, we were both on our feet and squared up in our individual fighting stances. Subconsciously, I was looking for a place to land my first punch because I wasn't one for all the lip-boxing bullshit and no bitch could talk reckless to me.

"What the fuck do you two think you're doing?" Erin asked.

I hadn't noticed her come back into the room, and I only looked at her now through my peripheral vision because I wasn't about to sleep on Kali. She was smaller than me, but I could see the fight in her eyes.

"I asked you two goofy bitches a question," Erin said more aggressively.

"Who you calling goofy? You better be talking to her with that shit," Kali said, still not taking a step back or lowering her guard.

"YOU'RE the goofy bitch, Kali! You blew this whole fucking thing out of proportion when I was just trying to have a conversation about my dad."

"And that's the problem. I'm trying to fuck YOU, you silly bitch, but you wanna keep questioning me like I'm trying to suck and fuck HIM. Damn, maybe I should, because that dick did look good enough to devour every meal of the day, and go back for dessert when the sweet tooth hits."

I could feel my mouth drop open in disbelief of the disrespect that had just escaped this bitch's mouth, but I was slower on the reaction than Erin was. Out of the corner of my eye, I saw Erin pull a mean-looking .22 with a banana clip out from behind her back.

"Bitch, what the fuck did you just say? Say it again and I'ma put a few holes in your face to give my man options on which one he can put his dick in."

The self-satisfied taunting look suddenly vanished from Kali's face as she took a step back to increase the distance between her and us.

"I-I didn't mean that towards you, Erin," Kali stammered.

"Didn't you though? Were you not speaking about my baby daddy like he's up for grabs, you disrespectful little hoe?"

"Hold up, because if you wanna be real, Leroy has only been your baby daddy for as long as he's been Lia's actual daddy. Last time that I checked, he was my mom's husband, and you're somebody else's wife."

"Little girl, before Leroy was your mom's anything, me and this good pussy were in his life, and we'll still be here after he divorces her ass. Be grateful that I allowed him to save that hoe because I could've, and should've, left her for dead," Erin replied in a politely nasty tone.

Before Kali could say anything else, the sounds of a motorcycle caught all of our attention, and immediately we knew who it was. The tension in the air went up by a few degrees, but I didn't see a way of defusing the shit at this point because Erin still had her gun out.

"Why your mouth stop moving? The man you had so much to say about will be in your presence in a few minutes, along with his WIFE, and I want you to keep that same energy you had," Erin stated, smiling.

Kali didn't say shit in response, but truthfully, I hadn't expected her to. We were silently counting the seconds in our minds once the sounds of the engine died, and then I saw him coming through the door with Gini in tow. I watched him assess the situation with one sweep of his eyes from left to right, and then he moved instinctively towards Erin.

"Is everything good?" he asked.

"Right as rain, just a little girl talk," Erin replied.

"Mom," Kali said, turning and stepping into the open arms of Gini.

Gini held her daughter close, but her eyes tracked a similar pattern as my dad's, and they landed squarely on the gun gripped in Erin's hand. I couldn't hear what Gini said when she leaned in and put her lips to Kali's ear, but that feeling in my stomach was back with a vengeance. Erin and my dad were talking in hushed tones amongst themselves, which was why they weren't paying attention to the temperature in the air, but I could feel the hint of a cold draft. Kali's eyes flickered to mine briefly, but I couldn't read what was in them because she suddenly switched positions and she was standing behind Gini.

"Leroy, you need to come over here," Gini said.

"Give me a minute," he replied.

"No...now," Gini demanded.

The tone of her voice didn't raise, but the threat in it could be heard by anyone with ears. My dad looked over his shoulder in annoyance, but he still didn't step away from Erin.

"I'm in the middle of a conversation, so just be patient," he said.

"The fuck I look like waiting for you to finish talking to another bitch like you ain't MY husband? Tell that hoe to wait."

"Excuse me?" Erin asked immediately.

"Hold up, because we ain't even 'bout to start this shit right now. Gini, you and I just talked about this, so don't start tripping all of a sudden," he interjected quickly.

"Are you referring to the conversation we had after we fucked like animals in the shower? Yeah, we talked, but I didn't agree to a muthafuckin' thing, especially not coming second to your side bitch."

"Okay, so first of all, if you were trying to get my attention by telling me that you fucked Leroy, then I'm sorry to tell you that I'm not impressed. 9 times out of 10 you probably sucked his dick too because I know that I personally LOVE to do that shit, and if you did, then you would've tastes my pussy and ass on it. So congratulations, you've had BOTH of us inside your trifling ass. Secondly, I've known this man way too long to ever fit into the category of a side bitch, sweety. I'm the bitch that keeps his secrets: the loyal bitch, the bitch that's about to give him a beautiful baby boy because that's what I DO. I'm the bitch you'll NEVER be, and that's what you need to remember when it comes to placement in Leroy's life. I'm permanent; you're just a rental. And if you REALLY know this man, then you'd know that it would be physically impossible for him to still be with you.

Sure, he could fuck you, but that makes you a cum dumpster, not a wife," Erin said, smirking victoriously.

The draft that I'd felt was now the breeze blowing off of Antarctica, and there was no hope for warmth. My eyes had played tennis for awhile between Erin and Gini, but they final led settled on Gini because a smirk had started to appear on her face as Erin was talking. At first, I didn't notice her hands go behind her back, but when I spotted movement between her and Kali I instinctively reached for the comfort of the pistol at the small of my back. Before I could open my mouth to issue any type of warning, I saw the gun appear in Gini's hand, which made me pull my own.

"Dad."

He glanced at me, saw my gun, and then looked to Gini where he spotted the same thing I had. This caused him to turn all the way around so that he was facing Gini, and he was in between her and Erin.

"What the fuck are YOU doing?" he asked.

"About to shut that bitch up behind you, as soon as you step out of the way."

I recognized the Taurus P365 9mm in Gini's grip, and I knew it was given to her by Kali, which complicated my emotions even more.

"You know that I'm not gonna step out of the way, so you might as well put the gun away and chill out with all the crazy shit," he replied.

"So you're just gonna let her disrespect me like that, Leroy? Okay, so you must be willing to die for the bitch too," Gini said, raising the gun.

My gun came up and was aimed at Gini out of instinct, and Erin tried to maneuver around my dad so that she could get her gun up, but he stopped her by blocking her with his body.

"Without a question I'm willing to give my life for hers and that of our unborn child, but are you willing to give your life in return?" he asked calmly.

Gini's eyes briefly flickered in my direction, and I saw no fear, which made me slide my finger inside the trigger guard while simultaneously releasing the safety. This shit was feeling like an old western, and I found myself praying silently for God to intervene because I didn't wanna have to do this.

"Give my life, Leroy? Well, what is my life without you, huh? Til death do us part, right?"

"You still have me in your life, Gini. Things are just different now. Put the gun down and let's work this out like we agreed back in the hotel room," he replied reasonably.

"We didn't agree. You laid it out for me to accept like you ALWAYS do, so fuck that shit. There's only one thing we ever really agreed upon, Leroy. Til death do us part," Gini said softly.

And then she pulled the trigger. She managed to get off a double tap before I planted a bullet in her left eye socket and adjusted my sights to Kali, who was trying to duck for cover. I put three bullets in Kali's chest, stopping her breathing, before dropping my gun and running over to my dad. Erin had him in her arms, and she was sobbing uncontrollably. There was so much I wanted to say before it was too late, but when I looked down into his eyes, I knew that my dad was beyond hearing my voice. All I could do was weep with regret.

# CHAPTER 21

*Erin*
*17 months later*

"Leroy Junior, I know that you're too young to understand how hard this last year and a half has been on your mommy, but one day I'll have to tell you. I'll have to tell you all the great things I know about your dad, and some of things I'd wished he could've escaped. Most of all though, I'll tell you every day about his love for you and for me. That's my promise to you, on this, your first birthday. Okay? I know you won't get it now, but I'm gonna read something I wrote for your daddy because every time I look at you, I see him," I said, pulling the flower cover notebook from his diaper bag.

The look in his eyes as he played with his feet and laughed in the bright afternoon sunshine took some of the heaviness off of my heart. LJ was a happy baby, and I intended to keep him that way, but the truth was unavoidable. One day I'd have to tell him a story that sounded so crazy it might give him nightmares, but the truth had to come from me first. Today wasn't that day though, so today he would hear only love spoken from my lips. Deep, unconditional, once in a lifetime, love...

"Are you ready, little man? This poem is titled STILL WITH YOU, and it goes like this...

Married to you mentally makes cheating an impossibility simply because there's no one who is as stimulating. Any evaluation is quickly viewed as nothing more than a carbon copy, sloppily put together. It's better for me to miss you as I do than to lie like this new view is as captivating. Appreciation for all men doesn't waver, but you're a different flavor that has stayed on my tongue long after you dissolved physically. Ceasing to be in this moment for the touching has only heightened my belief that our coupling is electricity multiplying. Makes me ache for that ride you promised me that one time. Still, patiently I wait with the weight of your love applying pressure to my chest plate, creating the sweetest sensations in the seconds between thoughts of you. Sometimes knowing what I ought to do don't make loving you from a distance easy, believe me, but defeat is a word I do not know. My mind and heart are invested in showing you that endurance is my influence so that you can see that like Jack, I'll never let go. See me as your Rose, and continue to love me through my individual journey, knowing that sooner rather than later I'll reappear magically. Anchor me in your waters because you remember how deeply we felt when we were allowed freedom of expression, and take with it this lesson. The best of us is yet to come, so coming undone by struggling makes as much sense as the moon daring the sun not to shine. You're mine and I'm yours, for all time, because anything less would be uncivilized... "

THE END

**Lock Down Publications and Ca$h Presents**
**Assisted Publishing Packages**

| **BASIC PACKAGE**<br>$499<br>Editing<br>Cover Design<br>Formatting | **UPGRADED PACKAGE**<br>$800<br>Typing<br>Editing<br>Cover Design<br>Formatting |
|---|---|
| **ADVANCE PACKAGE**<br>$1,200<br>Typing<br>Editing<br>Cover Design<br>Formatting<br>Copyright registration<br>Proofreading<br>Upload book to Amazon | **LDP SUPREME PACKAGE**<br>$1,500<br>Typing<br>Editing<br>Cover Design<br>Formatting<br>Copyright registration<br>Proofreading<br>Set up Amazon account<br>Upload book to Amazon<br>Advertise on LDP, Amazon and Facebook Page |

***Other services available upon request.
Additional charges may apply

**Lock Down Publications**
P.O. Box 944
Stockbridge, GA 30281-9998
Phone: 470 303-9761

# Submission Guideline

Submit the first three chapters of your completed manuscript to ldpsubmissions@gmail.com, subject line: Your book's title. The manuscript must be in a .doc file and sent as an attachment. Document should be in Times New Roman, double spaced and in size 12 font. Also, provide your synopsis and full contact information. If sending multiple submissions, they must each be in a separate email.

Have a story but no way to send it electronically? You can still submit to LDP/Ca$h Presents. Send in the first three chapters, written or typed, of your completed manuscript to:

LDP: Submissions Dept
Po Box 944
Stockbridge, Ga 30281

*DO NOT send original manuscript. Must be a duplicate.*

Provide your synopsis and a cover letter containing your full contact information.

Thanks for considering LDP and Ca$h Presents.

# NEW RELEASES

BLOODLINE OF A SAVAGE
BY PRINCE A. TAUHID
THE MURDER QUEENS 4
BY MICHAEL GALLON
THE BUTTERFLY MAFIA
BY FUMIYA PAYNE
KING KILLA 2
BY VINCENT "VITTO" HOLLOWAY
BABY, I'M WINTERTIME COLD 3
BY MEESHA
THESE VICIOUS STREETS
BY PRINCE A. TAUHID
TIL DEATH 2
BY ARYANNA
CITY OF SMOKE 2
BY MOLOTTI
PRODUCT OF THE STREETS
BY DEMOND "MONEY" ANDERSON
STEPPERS
BY KING RIO
THE LANE
BY KEN-KEN SPENCE
MONEY GAME 2
BY SMOOVE DOLLA
THE BLACK DIAMOND CARTEL
BY SAYNOMORE
CRIME BOSS 2
BY PLAYA RAY
THE BIRTH OF A GANGSTER 4
BY DELMONT PLAYER
THUG OF SPADES
BY COREY ROBINSON
LOVE IN THE TRENCHES 2
BY COREY ROBINSON
TIL DEATH 3
BY ARYANNA

# Available Now

BLOOD OF A BOSS **VI**
SHADOWS OF THE GAME II
TRAP BASTARD II
By Askari
LOYAL TO THE GAME **IV**
By T.J. & Jelissa
TRUE SAVAGE **VIII**
MIDNIGHT CARTEL IV
DOPE BOY MAGIC IV
CITY OF KINGZ III
NIGHTMARE ON SILENT AVE II
THE PLUG OF LIL MEXICO II
CLASSIC CITY II
By Chris Green
BLAST FOR ME **III**
A SAVAGE DOPEBOY III
CUTTHROAT MAFIA III
DUFFLE BAG CARTEL VII
HEARTLESS GOON VI
By Ghost
A HUSTLER'S DECEIT III
KILL ZONE II
BAE BELONGS TO ME III
TIL DEATH II
By Aryanna
KING OF THE TRAP III
By T.J. Edwards
GORILLAZ IN THE BAY V
3X KRAZY III
STRAIGHT BEAST MODE III
De'Kari
KINGPIN KILLAZ IV

STREET KINGS III
PAID IN BLOOD III
CARTEL KILLAZ IV
DOPE GODS III
Hood Rich
SINS OF A HUSTLA II
ASAD
YAYO V
Bred In The Game 2
S. Allen
THE STREETS WILL TALK II
By Yolanda Moore
SON OF A DOPE FIEND III
HEAVEN GOT A GHETTO III
SKI MASK MONEY III
By Renta
LOYALTY AIN'T PROMISED III
By Keith Williams
I'M NOTHING WITHOUT HIS LOVE II
SINS OF A THUG II
TO THE THUG I LOVED BEFORE II
IN A HUSTLER I TRUST II
By Monet Dragun
QUIET MONEY IV
EXTENDED CLIP III
THUG LIFE IV
By Trai'Quan
THE STREETS MADE ME IV
By Larry D. Wright
IF YOU CROSS ME ONCE III
ANGEL V
By Anthony Fields
THE STREETS WILL NEVER CLOSE IV
By K'ajji
HARD AND RUTHLESS III

KILLA KOUNTY IV
By Khufu
MONEY GAME III
By Smoove Dolla
JACK BOYS VS DOPE BOYS IV
A GANGSTA'S QUR'AN V
COKE GIRLZ II
COKE BOYS II
LIFE OF A SAVAGE V
CHI'RAQ GANGSTAS V
SOSA GANG III
BRONX SAVAGES II
BODYMORE KINGPINS II
By Romell Tukes
MURDA WAS THE CASE III
Elijah R. Freeman
AN UNFORESEEN LOVE IV
BABY, I'M WINTERTIME COLD III
By Meesha

QUEEN OF THE ZOO III
By Black Migo
CONFESSIONS OF A JACKBOY III
By Nicholas Lock
KING KILLA II
By Vincent "Vitto" Holloway
BETRAYAL OF A THUG III
By Fre$h
THE MURDER QUEENS III
By Michael Gallon
THE BIRTH OF A GANGSTER III
By Delmont Player
TREAL LOVE II
By Le'Monica Jackson
FOR THE LOVE OF BLOOD III

By Jamel Mitchell
RAN OFF ON DA PLUG II
By Paper Boi Rari
HOOD CONSIGLIERE III
By Keese
PRETTY GIRLS DO NASTY THINGS II
By Nicole Goosby
PROTÉGÉ OF A LEGEND III
LOVE IN THE TRENCHES II
By Corey Robinson
IT'S JUST ME AND YOU II
By Ah'Million
FOREVER GANGSTA III
By Adrian Dulan
GORILLAZ IN THE TRENCHES II
By SayNoMore
THE COCAINE PRINCESS VIII
By King Rio
CRIME BOSS II
Playa Ray
LOYALTY IS EVERYTHING III
Molotti
HERE TODAY GONE TOMORROW II
By Fly Rock
REAL G'S MOVE IN SILENCE II
By Von Diesel
GRIMEY WAYS IV
By Ray Vinci
RESTRAINING ORDER **I & II**
By CA$H & Coffee
LOVE KNOWS NO BOUNDARIES **I II & III**
By Coffee
RAISED AS A GOON I, II, III & IV
BRED BY THE SLUMS I, II, III
BLAST FOR ME I & II

Aryanna

ROTTEN TO THE CORE I II III

A BRONX TALE I, II, III

DUFFLE BAG CARTEL I II III IV V VI

HEARTLESS GOON I II III IV V

A SAVAGE DOPEBOY I II

DRUG LORDS I II III

CUTTHROAT MAFIA I II

KING OF THE TRENCHES

By Ghost

LAY IT DOWN **I & II**

LAST OF A DYING BREED I II

BLOOD STAINS OF A SHOTTA I & II III

By Jamaica

LOYAL TO THE GAME I II III

LIFE OF SIN I, II III

By TJ & Jelissa

BLOODY COMMAS I & II

SKI MASK CARTEL I II & III

KING OF NEW YORK I II,III IV V

RISE TO POWER I II III

COKE KINGS I II III IV V

BORN HEARTLESS I II III IV

KING OF THE TRAP I II

By T.J. Edwards

IF LOVING HIM IS WRONG…I & II

LOVE ME EVEN WHEN IT HURTS I II III

By Jelissa

WHEN THE STREETS CLAP BACK I & II III

THE HEART OF A SAVAGE I II III IV

MONEY MAFIA I II

LOYAL TO THE SOIL I II III

By Jibril Williams

A DISTINGUISHED THUG STOLE MY HEART I II & III

LOVE SHOULDN’T HURT I II III IV

RENEGADE BOYS I II III IV

PAID IN KARMA I II III
SAVAGE STORMS I II III
AN UNFORESEEN LOVE I II III
BABY, I'M WINTERTIME COLD I II
By Meesha
A GANGSTER'S CODE I &, II III
A GANGSTER'S SYN I II III
THE SAVAGE LIFE I II III
CHAINED TO THE STREETS I II III
BLOOD ON THE MONEY I II III
A GANGSTA'S PAIN I II III
By J-Blunt
PUSH IT TO THE LIMIT
By Bre' Hayes
BLOOD OF A BOSS I, II, III, IV, V
SHADOWS OF THE GAME
TRAP BASTARD
By Askari
THE STREETS BLEED MURDER **I, II & III**
THE HEART OF A GANGSTA I II& III
By Jerry Jackson
CUM FOR ME I II III IV V VI VII VIII
An LDP Erotica Collaboration
BRIDE OF A HUSTLA **I II & II**
THE FETTI GIRLS **I, II& III**
CORRUPTED BY A GANGSTA I, II III, IV
BLINDED BY HIS LOVE
THE PRICE YOU PAY FOR LOVE I, II ,III
DOPE GIRL MAGIC I II III
By Destiny Skai
WHEN A GOOD GIRL GOES BAD
By Adrienne
THE COST OF LOYALTY I II III
By Kweli
A GANGSTER'S REVENGE **I II III & IV**

THE BOSS MAN'S DAUGHTERS I II III IV V
A SAVAGE LOVE **I & II**
BAE BELONGS TO ME I II
A HUSTLER'S DECEIT I, II, III
WHAT BAD BITCHES DO I, II, III
SOUL OF A MONSTER I II III
KILL ZONE
A DOPE BOY'S QUEEN I II III
TIL DEATH
By Aryanna
A KINGPIN'S AMBITON
A KINGPIN'S AMBITION **II**
I MURDER FOR THE DOUGH
By Ambitious
TRUE SAVAGE I II III IV V VI VII
DOPE BOY MAGIC I, II, III
MIDNIGHT CARTEL I II III
CITY OF KINGZ I II
NIGHTMARE ON SILENT AVE
THE PLUG OF LIL MEXICO II
CLASSIC CITY
By Chris Green
A DOPEBOY'S PRAYER
By Eddie "Wolf" Lee
THE KING CARTEL **I, II & III**
By Frank Gresham
THESE NIGGAS AIN'T LOYAL **I, II & III**
By Nikki Tee
GANGSTA SHYT **I II &III**
By CATO
THE ULTIMATE BETRAYAL
By Phoenix
Boss'n Up i , ii & IIi
By Royal Nicole
I LOVE YOU TO DEATH

By Destiny J
I RIDE FOR MY HITTA
I STILL RIDE FOR MY HITTA
By Misty Holt
LOVE & CHASIN' PAPER
By Qay Crockett
TO DIE IN VAIN
SINS OF A HUSTLA
By ASAD
BROOKLYN HUSTLAZ
By Boogsy Morina
BROOKLYN ON LOCK I & II
By Sonovia
GANGSTA CITY
By Teddy Duke
A DRUG KING AND HIS DIAMOND I & II III
A DOPEMAN'S RICHES
HER MAN, MINE'S TOO I, II
CASH MONEY HO'S
THE WIFEY I USED TO BE I II
PRETTY GIRLS DO NASTY THINGS
By Nicole Goosby
TRAPHOUSE KING **I II & III**
KINGPIN KILLAZ I II III
STREET KINGS I II
PAID IN BLOOD **I II**
CARTEL KILLAZ I II III
DOPE GODS I II
By Hood Rich
LIPSTICK KILLAH **I, II, III**
CRIME OF PASSION I II & III
FRIEND OR FOE I II III
By Mimi
STEADY MOBBN' **I, II, III**
THE STREETS STAINED MY SOUL I II III

By Marcellus Allen
WHO SHOT YA **I, II, III**
SON OF A DOPE FIEND I II
HEAVEN GOT A GHETTO I II
SKI MASK MONEY I II
Renta
GORILLAZ IN THE BAY **I II III IV**
TEARS OF A GANGSTA I II
3X KRAZY I II
STRAIGHT BEAST MODE I II
DE'KARI
TRIGGADALE I II III
MURDAROBER WAS THE CASE I II
Elijah R. Freeman
GOD BLESS THE TRAPPERS I, II, III
THESE SCANDALOUS STREETS I, II, III
FEAR MY GANGSTA I, II, III IV, V
THESE STREETS DON'T LOVE NOBODY I, II
BURY ME A G I, II, III, IV, V
A GANGSTA'S EMPIRE I, II, III, IV
THE DOPEMAN'S BODYGAURD I II
THE REALEST KILLAZ I II III
THE LAST OF THE OGS I II III
Tranay Adams
THE STREETS ARE CALLING
Duquie Wilson
MARRIED TO A BOSS I II III
By Destiny Skai & Chris Green
KINGZ OF THE GAME I II III IV V VI VII
CRIME BOSS
Playa Ray
SLAUGHTER GANG I II III
RUTHLESS HEART I II III
By Willie Slaughter
FUK SHYT

By Blakk Diamond
DON'T F#CK WITH MY HEART I II
By Linnea
ADDICTED TO THE DRAMA I II III
IN THE ARM OF HIS BOSS II
By Jamila
YAYO I II III IV
A SHOOTER'S AMBITION I II
BRED IN THE GAME
By S. Allen
TRAP GOD I II III
RICH $AVAGE I II III
MONEY IN THE GRAVE I II III
By Martell Troublesome Bolden
FOREVER GANGSTA I II
GLOCKS ON SATIN SHEETS I II
By Adrian Dulan
TOE TAGZ I II III IV
LEVELS TO THIS SHYT I II
IT'S JUST ME AND YOU
By Ah'Million
KINGPIN DREAMS I II III
RAN OFF ON DA PLUG
By Paper Boi Rari
CONFESSIONS OF A GANGSTA I II III IV
CONFESSIONS OF A JACKBOY I II
By Nicholas Lock
I'M NOTHING WITHOUT HIS LOVE
SINS OF A THUG
TO THE THUG I LOVED BEFORE
A GANGSTA SAVED XMAS
IN A HUSTLER I TRUST
By Monet Dragun
CAUGHT UP IN THE LIFE I II III
THE STREETS NEVER LET GO I II III

By Robert Baptiste
NEW TO THE GAME I II III
MONEY, MURDER & MEMORIES I II III
By Malik D. Rice
LIFE OF A SAVAGE I II III IV
A GANGSTA'S QUR'AN I II III IV
MURDA SEASON I II III
GANGLAND CARTEL I II III
CHI'RAQ GANGSTAS I II III IV
KILLERS ON ELM STREET I II III
JACK BOYZ N DA BRONX I II III
A DOPEBOY'S DREAM I II III
JACK BOYS VS DOPE BOYS I II III
COKE GIRLZ
COKE BOYS
SOSA GANG I II
BRONX SAVAGES
BODYMORE KINGPINS
By Romell Tukes
LOYALTY AIN'T PROMISED I II
By Keith Williams
QUIET MONEY I II III
THUG LIFE I II III
EXTENDED CLIP I II
A GANGSTA'S PARADISE
By Trai'Quan
THE STREETS MADE ME I II III
By Larry D. Wright
THE ULTIMATE SACRIFICE I, II, III, IV, V, VI
KHADIFI
IF YOU CROSS ME ONCE I II
ANGEL I II III IV
IN THE BLINK OF AN EYE
By Anthony Fields
THE LIFE OF A HOOD STAR

By Ca$h & Rashia Wilson
THE STREETS WILL NEVER CLOSE I II III
By K'ajji
CREAM I II III
THE STREETS WILL TALK
By Yolanda Moore
NIGHTMARES OF A HUSTLA I II III
By King Dream
CONCRETE KILLA I II III
VICIOUS LOYALTY I II III
By Kingpen
HARD AND RUTHLESS I II
MOB TOWN 251
THE BILLIONAIRE BENTLEYS I II III
REAL G'S MOVE IN SILENCE
By Von Diesel
GHOST MOB
Stilloan Robinson
MOB TIES I II III IV V VI
SOUL OF A HUSTLER, HEART OF A KILLER I II
GORILLAZ IN THE TRENCHES
By SayNoMore
BODYMORE MURDERLAND I II III
THE BIRTH OF A GANGSTER I II
By Delmont Player
FOR THE LOVE OF A BOSS
By C. D. Blue
MOBBED UP I II III IV
THE BRICK MAN I II III IV V
THE COCAINE PRINCESS I II III IV V VI VII
By King Rio
KILLA KOUNTY I II III IV
By Khufu
MONEY GAME I II
By Smoove Dolla

A GANGSTA'S KARMA I II III
By FLAME
KING OF THE TRENCHES I II III
by GHOST & TRANAY ADAMS
QUEEN OF THE ZOO I II
By Black Migo
GRIMEY WAYS I II III
By Ray Vinci
XMAS WITH AN ATL SHOOTER
By Ca$h & Destiny Skai
KING KILLA
By Vincent "Vitto" Holloway
BETRAYAL OF A THUG I II
By Fre$h
THE MURDER QUEENS I II
By Michael Gallon
TREAL LOVE
By Le'Monica Jackson
FOR THE LOVE OF BLOOD I II
By Jamel Mitchell
HOOD CONSIGLIERE I II
By Keese
PROTÉGÉ OF A LEGEND I II
LOVE IN THE TRENCHES
By Corey Robinson
BORN IN THE GRAVE I II III
By Self Made Tay
MOAN IN MY MOUTH
By XTASY
TORN BETWEEN A GANGSTER AND A GENTLEMAN
By J-BLUNT & Miss Kim
LOYALTY IS EVERYTHING I II
Molotti
HERE TODAY GONE TOMORROW
By Fly Rock

# PILLOW PRINCESS
By S. Hawkins

# BOOKS BY LDP'S CEO, CA$H

TRUST IN NO MAN
TRUST IN NO MAN 2
TRUST IN NO MAN 3
BONDED BY BLOOD
SHORTY GOT A THUG
THUGS CRY
THUGS CRY 2
THUGS CRY 3
TRUST NO BITCH
TRUST NO BITCH 2
TRUST NO BITCH 3
TIL MY CASKET DROPS
RESTRAINING ORDER
RESTRAINING ORDER 2
IN LOVE WITH A CONVICT
LIFE OF A HOOD STAR
XMAS WITH AN ATL SHOOTER

www.ingramcontent.com/pod-product-compliance
Lightning Source LLC
Chambersburg PA
CBHW070013120626
46591CB00026B/281